A m. setting
not trans.

JP6- / 72

The Grand Street Collector

# The Grand Street Collector

*A Novel by*
JOSEPH ARLEO

WALKER AND COMPANY
New York

THE GRAND STREET COLLECTOR is a novel based on the assassination of Carlo Tresca. It is a work of fiction, not an historical document, and all the characters and events portrayed in it are fictitious.

First published in the United States of America in 1970 by the Walker Publishing Company, Inc.

Published simultaneously in Canada by The Ryerson Press, Toronto.

Library of Congress Catalog Card Number: 73-103857

Printed in the United States of America

The Grand Street Collector

# CHAPTER 1

IN THE VILLAGE OF MASINALTO, it had not rained for two
months. The fountain in the piazza had been dry three
weeks. It would never have happened in the days of Mussolini, old men murmured to each other, and the women
balanced stone water jars on their heads two kilometers
to the spring by the shrine of Christ at the edge of the
national highway, N19 on the Hallwag Motoring Map of
Italy.

Now there is considerable local traffic on that highway to Salerno—automobiles, scooters, trucks, buses
sometimes; but only once in the memory of Annunziata
Cafone, and not since the end of the war when the driver
of an Allied jeep relieved himself against a tree in
sight of Christ, had a stranger stopped at the way to
Masinalto. Not even a German tourist.

It was she, on that second Monday of September,
who saw the stranger standing by his open car at the
intersection of the roads. When he waved to her, Annunziata gazed at him in surprise and then returned her eyes
to the vessel she had come to fill, wondering what misfor-
tune the young man's presence signaled. Beware crossed

3

sticks and unexpected visits. She moved her jug under the rust-encrusted mouth of pipe and the trickling sound of water was suddenly joined by the starting roar of the car's engine. "Get going," she muttered, and looked up, expecting to see the stranger's tail heading north. Instead, the car had turned and was moving slowly toward her down the dirt road. Annunziata straightened up and swiftly crossed herself against the evil eye. She gathered her shawl about her as the car reached her and stopped.

The stranger smiled. "Buon giorno." He wore a necktie. The tips of his collar were fastened with tiny buttons to his white shirt.

"'Giorno."

"Is this the way to Masinalto?"

Annunziata nodded. He was young, between twenty-five and thirty, and nice looking, his face brown from the ride in the open car and not by a lifetime in the sun. What a shirt, she thought. He is not from the North, for he speaks in dialect. A spy for the police? These days?

"How far is it from here?"

"Two kilometers, around the curve." Annunziata pointed in the direction of Masinalto. When the stranger opened the door of his car, she saw the camera on the seat beside him. A tourist after all. But what business does he have in Masinalto?

The stranger undid the button at his throat and loosened his necktie, tucking it into his shirt as he moved Annunziata's jar from under the pipe. He splashed his face and wet his hair and then drank with his lips almost touching the pipe, like a peasant. Then he took a handkerchief from his pocket. It was the size of a tablecloth

4

and white like his good straight teeth. An American then? But the dialect?

"How good it tastes when you are thirsty, eh?"

Annunziata nodded. "See what it has done to the pipe."

"And how it has reduced mountains to pebbles on a beach," the stranger said with a smile. He dried his face on the handkerchief. "Tell me, is food to be had?"

Annunziata put the stone jar back under the trickle of water. "Some families eat three times a day."

"But can I find a dish of spaghetti? I begin to feel hunger."

"A bad year for flour, my friend. But you may find a piece of cheese or even a slice of salami. Wine we have in quantity." The jar was filled. She grabbed it up and in a single motion balanced it on her head.

"If you are going to Masinalto, I can take you in the car," the stranger said.

But what did he want? "Half the water would be spilled. Better to walk."

"Wait. Please."

Annunziata turned and looked at him. In spite of his fine car, he seemed afraid of being left alone, and Annunziata suddenly was sorry she had not been more kind. "What is it?" she asked. Was he running away from something? He had escaped to the right place: who would ever look for him in Masinalto?

"Do you know an old man who calls himself Natale Sbagliato?"

Wait a minute. Then this one *is* American. Annunziata lowered her hands to her side. Don Natale. Who did not know him? Was it possible that after all these years the Americans still had interest in him? Since years before the war? And yet, it could be. "Sbagliato?" For the second time, Annunziata began to walk away. "There is no one here who calls himself by that name."

The stranger touched her arm gently. "Please. Unless he died in the past few months, I know he is in Masinalto."

"You are mistaken, brother mine."

The stranger smiled. "I am Sbagliato, but I am not mistaken."

"Eh?"

"Sbagliato is my father."

"Truly?"

The stranger nodded.

"How do you call yourself?" Annunziata demanded.

"Pietro, after the grandfather of my father, who was born in Masinalto and fought the war with Garibaldi."

"How many years does your father have?"

"Sixty-five, sixty-six."

"And his sister, how does she call herself?"

"Emilia, Zia Emilia," the stranger said. "She is mother to me."

"When did you lose your mother?"

"Six months after she gave me life." From his pocket the stranger took a wallet and slipped from it a faded photograph that showed a man in his mid-forties wearing a straw hat and a flower in his buttonhole. At his side, holding his hand, was a blond-curled boy in velvet pants and patent-leather shoes.

Annunziata let the picture lie in her hand. When she returned it to the stranger, she smiled for the first time and dried her eyes with her knuckles, like a man. "I had forgotten it existed," she said quietly. "I saw it a century ago, when it was first made. Your father sent it to us

6

with an early letter of America. We must have it still with papers in a drawer." Annunziata touched the stranger's face. "You have his eyes," she said, "but do not expect they will see him as he was a lifetime ago."

"Then he is here?"

"And where did you expect him to be? In Paradise? Don Natale keeps himself. Come, come with me now. You said you had hunger half hour ago."

They started out. Annunziata walked swiftly alongside the car, every twenty-five paces refusing the ride the stranger Pietro Sbagliato offered till finally he was convinced the jar she carried on her head was no encumbrance. "Look," she said after a while of silence, "all those questions before. If you are truly the son of Don Natale, you understand that it is for his own . . ."

"I understand."

They had made the curve, and below, in the morning sun, on the flat roofs of Masinalto, rocks anchoring loose tiles were like pomegranates drying on a corrugated tray. Annunziata pointed to a corner roof. "See there. It is your paternal house."

The stranger slowed the car till it barely moved. "That one, like all the others?"

"No better, but no worse. Did you expect Castel Gondolfo?"

"No, only . . ."

"You are used to the palaces of America. That house"—Annunziata glanced over her shoulder—"is good for another hundred years. Today Don Natale is sorry it is no longer in the family."

"Then it was sold?" the stranger asked quietly.

"Years and years ago, right after your grandfather died."

They moved along in silence now, only the car's

7

throaty hum and the crunching of stones beneath its tires keeping pace with Annunziata's breathing. Then Pietro Sbagliato asked, "And where does my father live today?"

"In a single downstairs room in that house of his birth. The present owner, a man with a good heart, though I cannot say it for his wife, lets him have it without rent. In memory of the old days."

"And how does he live?" The question was so softly put Annunziata barely heard the words.

She repressed a sigh and instead laughed aloud to buoy the spirits of the son of Don Natale. "The same as the rest of us. He has no magic touch. A little farming, a ten-dollar bill now and then from the other side. We manage to survive in Masinalto. You will see him soon yourself. But what of the others from this countryside who live now in America? Tell me of Teresa Fellini. Do you know her? At sixteen, when she left us, she could have taken a prize for her beauty."

"I too remember her beauty. Her hair is white now, and she is without teeth. She spends her days in church. She never took a husband."

"Truly? Ah, what a sin. She was made like a statue."

They talked of others from her youth, and then Annunziata rested her hand for balance on the door of the car as she walked downhill now, into the village. "Old age is a carrion," she said, and shut her eyes, walking blind a few steps, the car her guide. She opened her eyes and saw a woman stooped in a field. "It is the son of Don Natale," Annunziata called, "after twenty years to be united with his father."

The woman straightened up and kissed together the tips of her thumb and index finger as though she came

8

from the Stations of the Cross, then returned slowly to her work.

Time had deteriorated the stucco facade of the house, and the structural rubble stone stood exposed between the tattered edges of Communist posters plastered there like a patchwork quilt that brought small comfort. Pietro Sbagliato slowed the car again as they passed it in front, expecting the next moment would bring an old man to the scarred and battered door, but Annunziata said Don Natale would not return till sundown. Pietro glanced at his watch; the hour was just after one. A pair of chickens pecked without enthusiasm at a dried deposit of horse manure by the side of the road as the car went by, and Annunziata directed Pietro to turn right at the next viale.

The alley opened onto a cobbled square in whose center stood the fountain without water. Seated around its limestone rim, like boys fishing from a bridge, was a circle of men whose ages ranged, Pietro guessed, from sixteen to seventy. As the car approached, they followed it with their eyes, and when Annunziata announced he was the son of Natale Sbagliato from America, the oldest ones nodded their heads but did not speak. A young voice muttered, "Give him my regards."

There were three tables in the square, pressed against the shaded wall of a building, and four men played cards at one of them, puffing on dead cigars. The other tables were deserted. The shutters of an upstairs window on the square were suddenly thrown open, and Annunziata waved to the woman who appeared there

9

and called, "Amalia, come." And then another woman's face and Annunziata shouted, "It is the son of Don Natale," to which one of the cardplayers added, "Who comes in a hired car with pockets filled with money for us."

Women came and their men too, husbands and sons, with smiling faces and fresh-washed hands. They looked familiar to Pietro, and he recognized features that were part of his own physiognomy: the bold straight nose and squared-off jaw, the sleepy eyes and broad-lined forehead. He was a composite of all the faces he saw, and he smiled in recognition and they did too. He was one of them, and he warded off the invidious thought that but for fate, on that hot September afternoon in that arid village square, he too might have been witnessing the arrival of an American son.

The tallest man of the crowd stepped forward and clasped Pietro's hand. "I am your father's brother. Do you know of me? Giorgio?"

Pietro nodded. "I remember the name," he said, and then his uncle grabbed him roughly and kissed his face.

"How long do you remain with us?" Giorgio asked, drying his eyes on the cuffs of his shirt. "Forgive me, eh?"

"I return to Salerno tonight."

"Ah. So far for so short a stay. Pass three or four days with us."

"I must get back to my work in New York."

"Ah."

"What work do you do?" a man asked. "I remember your father from before he went to America."

Pietro shook the hand of his father's friend. "I teach the literature of Italy at a university."

10

"Bravo."

"Then you yourself have been to the university?"

"What a question! How could he teach at the university if he himself had not attended the university?"

"And who is the best writer of Italian books?"

Pietro smiled. "There are many . . ."

"But the very best, the first?"

"I do not know. Silone, Moravia?"

"Ah."

"Ah."

"Ah."

They had never heard the names before.

"But leave him alone now." Annunziata stopped their questions suddenly. "He asked to eat three hours ago and no one moves." She took Pietro by the arm and led him to a table away from the cardplayers whose game his presence had not disturbed.

A heavy wooden blind below a peeling sign TABACO CAFE rumbled up, and in two minutes a shy boy of ten or eleven set before Pietro an embroidered napkin and a pitcher of red wine. The boy came back with two glasses, a knife, and a chunk of provolone.

"Eat, Professor, eat," Giorgio Sbagliato urged, and he sat down across from Pietro and filled the two glasses. He raised his glass. "To the understanding between father and son," he said quietly. He lowered his eyes and drank.

No one spoke after that.

Then someone said, "Put a little more wine in his glass, Giorgio."

As he ate, they began to ask about the others who had gone to America from Masinalto years before. Someone had a nephew in Provvidenza. Pietro explained that city was far from New York. Most of their questions Annunziata answered with information he had given her earlier, and Pietro was free then to nod and consider once again the approaching interview with his father. His stomach tightened against the good hard cheese he ate, but he forced it down with mouthfuls of wine in order not to offend.

Across the square, a barefoot boy patted the bony head of a donkey. The boy reminded Pietro of himself in the picture he had shown to Annunziata. Three months after that picture was taken Don Natale Sbagliato, perfect father of his motherless child, carrying the respect and admiration of New York's entire Italian population —despite recent release from parole of a sentence imposed for collecting lottery coins on Manhattan's lower East Side, a respectable enough profession those days— on the evening of September 17, 1936, disappeared and was never seen again in America.

Giorgio Sbagliato filled the glass before him another time. "For an American, you know well the art of drinking wine, Professor."

"I learned from a master." Pietro drank off the glass and reached for the cigarette pack in his pocket. He offered it to Giorgio and then passed it along to the men and boys who had watched him eat. When it came back to him, there were two cigarettes left.

Giorgio rolled his cigarette delicately between his fingers. "A beautiful American cigarette."

Pietro pushed the nearly empty pack across the table. "Please. I have more."

"No no no no," Giorgio said, but he finally accepted, adding his cigarette to the two in the pack, which he put

12

in his pocket. "And how do you like our wine?" He made a face that said he himself did not think much of it.

"It is good." To prove he meant what he said, Pietro filled his glass again and everyone laughed. The boy who had brought the pitcher took it away for more.

"When you get used to it, it tastes like champagne," Giorgio said. "Our best wine we send to Salerno for a better price. Probably you have had more of it in New York than we have had here in the last twenty years."

"If it is true, I am sorry for it."

"Do not lose sleep over it, Professor," Giorgio Sbagliato said. "We do not know the difference between good wine and the bad anymore, and we have the extra money the good brings. We are content with this the way a man is content with his wife. He knows her faults, knows better women exist, and yet when he is thirsty . . . eh, Professor?"

"Look," Pietro said politely, "I am many grades below professor. I am an instructor."

One of the cardplayers finally spoke. "Si si si si si, but how would it be to call the son of Don Natale instructor?" he said without lifting his eyes from his hand.

Pietro disregarded the curl of sarcasm in the question. Then an ill-concealed laugh cracked from the cardplayer's partner. No one said anything.

"That is what I am."

The cardplayer cleared his throat and spat on the cobblestones of the square.

Pietro pushed his chair from the table and swung around as he stood up. "I take it you are not a friend of my father." His voice was loud but the cardplayer pretended not to have heard.

13

Giorgio reached across the table and touched Pietro's arm. "Forgive him," he said, "please. He lost a brother to the Fascists."

"I know the job Sbagliato did," the cardplayer said quietly, as if raising a bid.

Giorgio squeezed Pietro's arm. "They shot his youngest brother there, under the arch of the cafe," he explained swiftly, "the blood still stains the stones inside the door."

"And I lost a father to them. I am sorry for that one. That he remembers Fascism was not an American invention." Pietro took a fistful of crumbled thousand-lire notes from his pocket. "How much do I owe for the cheese and wine?"

"Please. Do not offend us."

"I have no wish to offend you." He put his money away. "I thank you for your kindness."

They made room for him as he turned toward the car for another pack of cigarettes. The rim of the fountain was deserted now, and when he reached the car, the cigarettes were gone and so was the camera. Discouraged, Pietro took the ignition key and headed slowly toward the road Annunziata had led him along. "I know the job Sbagliato did . . . I know the job Sbagliato did . . ."

The sight of the corner house returned to him like a sickness. He had edged it from his mind the past half hour. Now he was faced with it head on, and even the most generous stretch of his imagination could not accommodate the crippled hovel to the palazzo he had been led to believe in years before. As he went by, Pietro glanced up at the rusted iron grillwork that rimmed the little balcony outside a pair of double windows below the roof. A string of red peppers hung like giant rosary

14

beads from a broken finial on the rail. The wall around the window was pocked as if from shelling, but there had been no combat in Masinalto.

He walked on. Soon he reached the spring where he had first met the old woman. With nothing better to do as he waited for end of day, he stopped again at the pipe and rinsed his hands in the cool trickle of water and lowered his lips to the rusted mouth as he had done before. This time, when he looked up from his drink, his eyes caught the pale pink statue of Christ and its pedestal of natural rock. He hadn't seen it the first time there and now, for an instant, he thought it was a real man leaning against a tree. When he realized his mistake, a sudden impulse brought his hand to his face and he caught himself about to pray. "Oh God," he murmured, and then the instant passed. He walked a few steps closer to the statue. Flowers, the color of pumpkin, stemmed from a discarded tomato can at its feet. There was no water in the can. He looked more closely at the bright flowers and discovered they were made of straw. The Christ was cement, the flowers were fake. He looked up at the hand-painted face of the statue, at the broad-stroke patient smile that had weathered years of rain and sun. He found himself smiling back. "No thank you. No more for me," he said. He backed away and sat down on an outcropping of rock and patted all his pockets before remembering he was out of cigarettes.

"He is a very modest Christ, but He is ours," someone said behind him.

He turned around. Giorgio Sbagliato stood there, the stolen camera hanging from its strap around his shoulder. "He works miracles, too," he said with an embarrassed smile, and handed over the camera. "It does little good, I know, to apologize for the pigs who took it. And these." He turned in the fresh cigarettes that had disappeared from the car.

Pietro peeled away the red cellophane strip across the top of the pack. Giorgio stopped him. "Have one of mine," he said gently, and offered one of the two remaining cigarettes Pietro had given him earlier that afternoon. "Please."

They smoked in silence for a while, Giorgio examining his American cigarette after every puff, as though even the sight of the tightly rolled tobacco added to his enjoyment of it. "Excuse me," he said finally, "but why do you come now, after all these years?"

"If you have to ask I cannot answer."

"Ah, do not misunderstand," Giorgio said quietly. "Everyone here knows something of that affair, I more than the others."

"And how do you know so much?"

"Your father and I are brothers in the true sense of the word. There are no secrets between us."

Pietro looked up quickly. "Then he has confessed to you?"

"Confessed?" The older man pretended to be amused. "Thanks to that word, the priests live well. But they do not know its meaning."

"And . . ."

"I see the confession you have come to hear," Giorgio said.

Pietro shook his head. "For twenty years I have tightened my belt against it. That is why I have come here now. If you knew with what hope I am here—that my father's words will free him from the stories told by friends and enemies alike, conversations not meant for the ears of a child."

Giorgio dropped the butt of his cigarette and ground it with his shoe till the bit of paper and tobacco shreds disintegrated into the dust. "Free him." He mimicked Pietro's words. "And you."

"Yes," Pietro said, "and me. What do you think it has been to carry the weight of a father's guilt like a ton of stone for twenty years? Guilt, suspicion of guilt, it is all the same matter. I want it off my back—am I understood?—I want it off my back."

Giorgio nodded his head slowly. "How he has suffered for you," he said quietly. "But what can you know, Professor."

"What can I know?" Pietro asked. "I have had my lifetime till now to learn, to study for the examination of this evening." On the other side of the valley, the bells of a church tolled and the muffled clanging drifted across the peaceful air and reached him, lonely, as he said, suddenly gentle, "I know too much, *much* too much."

# CHAPTER 2

AT SIX-THIRTY on the evening of September 17, 1936, Colonello Alfonso Tedesco entered the lobby of the Savoy Plaza Hotel and crossed the polished marble floor. He went directly to the gold-grilled registration desk, set his single suitcase down, and waited for the clerk. An enormous rococo mirror above a fake Renaissance table invited his admiration, and he stepped back to catch his image in the glass, to run a hand through his straight dark hair.

He registered under the name Frank Panzini and gave an Albany address. In good English, he ordered a bottle of scotch and a bucket of ice to be sent upstairs immediately: if he was to be a rich American he would behave like one.

His rooms gave out on Fifth Avenue and afforded a fine view of Central Park. He could see a lake there, just inside the wall, and a rowboat sitting in the still water like a decoy. He undressed by the window, gazing down at the open-topped buses that rushed from corner to corner along the avenue, and when room service appeared with his bottle, gave away his suit to be pressed. He turned hot water on in the tub and removed his dressing gown. Naked, he poured himself a drink and roamed about the apartment examining the silk brocade of the drapery, the mahogany veneer of the furniture. In a bureau drawer he found a lady's hairpin which he tossed onto the coverlet of the double bed, near the pillow. Before stepping into his bath, he telephoned to have his shoes polished.

He lowered himself into his tub's warm water then till only his head was in the cool of the room. So far so good. He smiled, remembering the Customs officer on the dock and the salute elicited by his passport's stamp of the U.S. Embassy in Rome. The comfort of the water kept the smile on his lips as he considered the collector who was to do this job.

He knew the type well. These were the ones who litter the dusty piazzas of villages far below the belt of the peninsula while they curse the bone-dry misery of their lives from morning till night. Nursed along by the meager pap of money orders sent air mail by new American relatives, they hoard their subsistence till money enough is accumulated to desert the earth of their birth.

Then once in America, ah! The social clubs they establish, the airs they put on along with their first pair of shoes. And the employment they take—cutting hair, shining shoes, pressing clothes, serving food, sweeping streets, digging ditches, laying rail: the slave-labor of their Anglo-Saxon masters. But now this collector was ready for redemption. It would be seen.

From the start, his own intellect and intuition had dictated the selection of an expert to do this job. "Untried hands are never to be employed in matters of this kind," he had protested, "not under ideal conditions,

20

and certainly not in the present situation. The risk of scandal is enormous."

Rocco Gargatto had risen from his desk and cracked the knuckles of his big hands. "My dear Colonel Tedesco, I appreciate your opinion. But this is all mine. I have known him thirty years. Your desire to dissociate yourself from the case is understood and unchallenged. Now if you will simply follow your orders, all our ends will be served. Think of your part, if you like, as a pleasure trip to America."

"Five thousand dollars could bring home the severed parts of the pig," he had insisted. "I cannot believe that the instrument of the century's most powerful army is to be the hand of some immigrant collector."

Rocco had spun about in his slow walk across the study. "This is no ordinary collector. Remember that. For twelve years this man followed at my side. The success of my business in Chicago and New York, from 1920 to 1932, can be traced in great measure to his diligent efforts on my behalf. In his own way, the man is an artist—and a dear close friend. Is it understood, Colonel?"

"Yes," he had murmured, "it is understood. But excuse me. Why, if this man possesses such skill, has he been reduced to the collection of lottery centimes near the Bowery of New York?"

Rocco had smiled then. "The times are bad. Call it retirement if you will, and a desire for respectability. He is called 'Don.' I arranged the place for him before coming abroad. He has a son now, a handsome boy of six, for whom he lives. Only I know his longing to be truly big in the eyes of the boy, and to be of service to the country he left barefoot. He has no money. He will accept no charity. This job will bring alive his wildest dreams.

He will be a patriot. A rich one. His son will go to medical school. I offer him this assignment with my heart, the more so since the beast he strikes has it coming from me personally, as well as from Il Duce."

"And should he refuse?"

"He will not refuse, Colonel," Rocco had assured him. "You have my permission to convince him he must not refuse—for his own good and for the good of his country."

And so the job had been assigned. Tedesco sighed and raised his shoulders out of the water. "Very well," he said aloud. He began to wash.

As he soaped himself, he reviewed the time-table in his mind: at the Consulate before eight-thirty; the brief-case—money, passport, the automatic; downtown by train; Morrone's at nine-fifteen, the collector, his instructions; twelve-fifteen his decision, and one-thirty, finished—perhaps. Yes, finished. He rinsed himself and stood up, reaching for the thick white towel draped across the cane chair by the tub.


An hour later, at the Consulate, a uniformed guard, obeying general orders, refused to admit him beyond the last step of the vestibule till word was forwarded from upstairs that the gentleman at the gate was to be escorted to the library at once.

The Secretary was at his desk when Tedesco entered but rose immediately and rushed forward to greet him. "My dear Colonel. How does it go?"

"Without harm," Tedesco replied coldly.

"You must forgive our having kept you waiting

22

downstairs," the Secretary said. "One cannot be too secure these days."

Tedesco nodded. "Understood. How does it go?"

"Truly, on my part, I have no complaints, especially now that the demonstrations have ended. But how go things at home?"

Tedesco smiled now. "To perfection. You read the newspapers?" He raised his eyes to the portrait framed by silver and gold above the quattrocento chest opposite the door.

The Secretary returned to his desk. "I will not keep you." From his pocket he drew a key with which he unlocked the bottom drawer. "You were not followed, of course."

Tedesco did not answer but took up the small brown leather briefcase that was placed on the desk. He undid the latch. "The weapon is an American one."

"A forty-five caliber piece of Colt manufacture. With full clip."

Tedesco pocketed the automatic. "I pray to God this collector knows how it is operated," he said to himself. He took out a packet of bills two inches thick bound with a rubberband.

"Three thousand dollars," the Secretary said. "If you yourself have need . . ."

Tedesco shook his head. "Why two passports?" he asked suddenly as he emptied the briefcase.

"One for the boy."

"I was told nothing about the boy," Tedesco said angrily. "How can they expect me to be certain a six-year-old will do as he is told?"

The Secretary shook his head. "I am with you," he

23

said. "We received the order just the night before last. You would not believe what we went through just to photograph the child. With the father, the collector, it was a simple matter. Months ago, Rocco wrote to him and asked for one or two . . ."

"Enough. I am not interested in the mechanics of passport photography. What the devil, have I become a nursemaid now?"

The Secretary was silent.

"I make no promises for the boy."

"Excuse me, Colonel," the Secretary said quietly. "But the collector will not move without assurances for his son. Of this we are certain. I do not imagine it is seriously expected that the child would accompany him; it is more for appearances, if you understand me."

Tedesco sighed and nodded his head. "All right, all right." He stood up to leave. "The undertaker has been informed?"

"He waits for you at nine-and-a-quarter. All else has been arranged as planned." The Secretary extended his hand. "Good luck, Colonel," he said softly.

"Arrivederci."


The air was still and warm and not unlike an autumn evening in Rome. Had it not been for the consideration of the six-year-old, he would have been satisfied and really quite happy with the way things were proceeding. As he walked, the heavy pistol slapped against his thigh. So the collector was a proud pappa. Then, of course, the promise would be made that he would never be separated from his son: it was that simple.

He looked for a nickel in his handful of coins before

24

stepping down into the subway station at Lexington Avenue. He disliked traveling this way, but a taxi arriving on Grand Street would attract as much attention as a limousine. He knew the mentality of the people there.

This time he did not mind the ride. The roar and rumbling of the train, the force with which it slammed its passengers together and against the benches like so many sacks of potatoes, filled him at once with an envy of its mechanical perfection, and with the enthusiasm of a spectator waiting for a soccer game to begin. He thought too of the train ride he would take before Christmas with Il Duce and Rocco aboard the special cars being built for them now by the Jibuti–Addis Ababa Railway. Tonight he would not disappoint them; they had better not disappoint him: he had not yet been to Abyssinia.

The streets downtown were curiously deserted. No gnarled and twisted men with burnt-out bits of black cigars straddled chairs in darkened doorways, no bovine women with hairy lips stared from pillowed window sills, no undershirted children flashed with screams from between automobiles parked in the street, no card games under street lights, no cries or strident laughter from the rooms that rose from the chalked and splintered sidewalks.

He quickened his step. A confusion of voices and sounds seemed to roll forward to greet him. As the noises swelled, Tedesco realized that Mulberry Street, as it crossed Grand a few blocks up ahead, was bridged from one sidewalk to the other by a great arch of red and green lights high above the street. Suddenly a drum rolled. Discordant violins and cornets announced "The Soldiers' Chorus." Tedesco was around the corner by the time the final chord was struck, and as silence grabbed

25

the cymbals' clash, he came face to face with the Feast of San Gennaro, patron saint of Naples.

On either side of Grand, as far as he could see in either direction, Mulberry Street was panoplied under an arch of light that rivaled the vaulted ceiling of some al fresco Renaissance church. Buttressing tenement walls and wooden piers put up from the curb to support the colored lights transformed the sidewalks into cluttered aisles. There in those alleys, and in the street as well, canvas-covered concessionaires sold sizzling sandwiches of peppers and sausages, see-through wedges of pizza, sweating bottles of ice-cold beer, raffles for a frigidaire, paper cups of strawberry ice, sunflower seeds by a wooden measure, numbers on an oilcloth strip.

A pair of priests, a beggar, graying couples arm in arm, fascinated and nearly frightened foreigners in fur from the uptown city, young people yearning for darkness, widows mourning with bead-mumbling lips, a reed of a man threaded with bright balloons followed by the wide-eyed silent stare of children. And everywhere now, the incessant strains of the seventeen-piece brass band.

It was seated on a raised platform in the middle of the block. Members of the original group sported garrison caps purchased twenty years before, which, though discolored, were still of service, while the braided coats and navy trousers had been discarded as their owners spread with age. Only the first cornetist, obese when the uniform order first was placed, could stuff himself still into that tattered crimson cloth. The maestro wore a swallowtail coat and conducted with a baton as long as his arm.

There was no way to avoid the street. Tedesco lowered his eyes finally and hurried his step. When he looked up again, he was grateful for the cracked and peeling gilt

26

letters, serifs long ago gone, that spread across the center of the dark shop window to spell MORRONE'S FUNERAL PARLOR. He pushed open the plate glass door and a voice said softly, "I am honored, Colonel, honored."

"This lovely room makes one forget where one is," Tedesco said with a smile as he seated himself in the undertaker's office. The chimes of the clock in the outside corridor began to sound nine o'clock. "Tell me, Morrone, do you make a good living here?"

"Comfortable," the undertaker said. "Though things are somehow quiet during the Festa. It is as though the old and the sick respect the pleasure of the young and the well, and postpone their departures till life returns to normal." He went to the carved mahogany sideboard decked with a crystal bowl of apples and grapes. "Excuse me, Colonel." He opened one of the doors and from a shelf lined with glasses and decanters took a tall slim bottle and two stemmed snifters. "I remember your fondness of strega."

Tedesco bowed and placed his pack of Nazionale on the table. "Nor did I forget your taste for cigarettes."

They drank to the health and long life of Mussolini. Tedesco fitted a Nazionale to his ivory holder and then pushed the green pack across the table to Morrone. "Tell me, what is your opinion of this collector?" he asked.

"An honest enough collector," the undertaker answered.

"Do you trust him?"

"He paid twenty-five dollars on a win three weeks ago."

Tedesco poured and drank another glass of strega. "And his loyalty to the Government?"

"Unquestionable. The blind unbreakable faith of

ignorance," Morrone said. "But why this sudden interest in the collector? Why has he been asked to come here tonight? Is the Premier anxious to play a number?"

"In a certain sense." Tedesco smiled and nodded his head. He closed his eyes for a minute as though evaluating the advisability of gambling with the collector. "Do you know of his close bond with Rocco Gargatto?" he asked.

The undertaker laughed. "Rocco may have placed a bet with him years ago. But the collector would have you believe they are like brothers."

"You would find yourself better off believing that, Undertaker. The collector is modest when he speaks of Rocco's regard for him. Believe it, your collector and Rocco are like this." He crossed two fingers.

"Then I believe it," Morrone said. "Though it takes me by surprise."

"The surprises have not yet started," Tedesco said. He slid the bottle across the table. "Take yourself another drink. I come to tell you a story."

A dull edge of fear began to touch the back of the undertaker's neck as he watched Tedesco loosen his black silk tie and undo the gold button at the throat, as though the story he was about to hear would uncoil like a snake from beneath the starched collar.

A gentle knock at the door postponed the colonel's speech. Morrone glanced at his wristwatch and nodded.

"A man of great courage, it can be seen," Tedesco muttered. "Let him come."

The undertaker stood up. "Enter."

# CHAPTER 3

Don Natale the Collector had slept poorly the night before. Twice he had been awakened by the illusion of someone calling his name from the hallway downstairs. When he dozed off the third time, the sky between the vertical edge of the shade and the window frame had been the pale blue of early morning. And then he had dreamed.

He was dressed in the uniform of a Bersagliere captain, the plume of his beret bowed in the breeze. He led a parade. By his side, in uniform too, Rocco marched. The line of march was the Via dei Imperiali. But he was not marching, he was astride a white stallion. Before the steps of the Quirinal Palace, Il Duce waited to bestow upon him the Order of Annunziata, making him a cousin of the King.

The collector edged his legs over the side of his bed. Today was the day. It was also San Gennaro's day. "San Gennaro, help me," he prayed in daylight, "help me in whatever thing this is that Rocco wants. For is it truly possible? Truly do I have still his trust—*today*, that he is who he is? *The American right hand of Mussolini.*" A sudden surge of joy flooded through him. "That of all those in this country he knows so well, I, *I* am the one he reaches for. That the brotherhood of suffering is undeniable. That the Eternal Father makes me worthy of Rocco's trust."

And then, with the enthusiasm of a man at last in hand with the opportunity dreamed of early in life, that opportunity whose fulfillment brings clear satisfaction of inmost soul and approbation of fellow man, that opportunity men grow old waiting to grasp—till finally, in full old age, it is fortunately forgotten, thus avoiding the misery of disappointed death, with the enthusiasm of such a man and given chance, Don Natale touched his feet to the cold floor and got out of bed.

His hand trembled as he shaved.

Dressed, in the kitchen, he set water to boil and cleared the table of Pietro's breakfast cup and crusts of bread. He moved aside Emilia's embroidery frame to get to the cupboard where the coffee was kept. He ground a handful of beans and sniffed the fresh coarse powder. Then he washed the pot, filled it, and waited by the window for the water to boil.

He sniffed the fresh mint and basil that ringed the red and yellow chrysanthemums in the box on the fire-escape, and for an instant was lost in the fields of his childhood. In the street below, a bright sun shone on women hovering about the pushcarts by the curb, choosing vegetables and watching the scale as the cartmen weighed.

The fish cart was at the corner. Natale saw Emilia hurry to it from the bakery. The fish-man held up silver fish for her to see—twice, three times before Emilia was satisfied. She opened her purse and held out money to the fish-man. He shook his head and threw the fish back to its

30

bin. Emilia thrust her money forward under his nose, as though to make him smell it. The fish-man wrapped the fish in newspaper, like flowers.

The water boiled. Natale poured it into the pot and took down a cup and saucer. The coffee was ready in a minute and he returned to the window.

"But why at Morrone's Funeral Parlor?" he asked himself. "Morrone, who robs us in death. Five hundred dollars for a coffin that costs him fifty." He glanced at the clock above the stove. He took the bread knife from the table drawer and sharpened a pencil out the window. He patted his breast pocket to be sure of the notebook. Then he went to the window one more time and took a yellow flower for the lapel of the brown suit he had chosen to wear that day.


The morning was like a courtesan waiting for the romance of evening. Overhead, the dull-colored bulbs' supporting poles and wires were the braces and stays of a sequin evening dress that would sparkle in the night, superstructure under which excitement would be made to flow.

Cold Natale hurried along, smoking his de Nobili.

"Buon giorno, Don Natale."

"Buon giorno, signora." Someone whose name slipped his mind; Natale touched the brim of his hat.

He waved his newspaper to the barber as he passed the barbershop. "Natale. Do not forget me today." the barber called. "I had a dream last night that will fix me good."

"I too had a dream, brother mine. Have I ever forgotten you?"

"I speak of today," the barber said.

31

Natale crossed the street. "Rocco Rocco Rocco Rocco," he hummed to himself, a fly at his own ear.

"A nice day, eh, Collector?"

"What do you say, Nat?"

He smiled. He nodded. He tipped his hat.

He took the ring of keys from his pocket and opened the door to the Lodge. He set his newspaper down by the head chair at the end of the long narrow table and pushed through the parted curtains to the back room.

He made more coffee.

He took two envelopes from the desk and put them by his newspaper. Then he sat down.

Sunlight through the store window before him like an X-ray revealed the vein-like imperfections of the gold lettering that spelled SONS OF ITALY 1922.

With his pencil, Natale crossed out the letterhead from the two envelopes. He wrote his initials in the remaining space above. Then from his wallet he took two single dollar bills and a five. He put the two dollars in one envelope, the five in the other. He marked the first envelope with a small *s* and sealed them both. He took his notebook from his pocket and turned to the last page. To the list of weekly notations under the heading POLIZIA he added "17 settembre 1936—2 e 5." Then he put the book away and unfolded his newspaper.

He read of Mussolini fortifying his physical energy with sulfur baths in the resort village of Tivoli where, after listening to the pleas of local women for light, the Premier caused the installation of electricity to begin four hours after the spontaneous request.

He read about Viceroy Graziani in Abyssinia prohibiting natives from crawling on their stomachs as a sign of obeisance to their Italian conquerors. "Italy desires her Ethiopian citizens to be free and have perfect con-

sciousness of their dignity as men," Graziani had pro-
claimed.

Natale looked up from his paper and gazed out into
the street. He thought of the Irish policeman who would
arrive soon, to take the envelopes on the table. If there
were some way of showing him these articles! But the
American newspapers did not print this news which
brought credit to the land they scorned. "Let them continue in their ignorance," Natale mused. "They will get a
shock one day." A sigh, a delicate thread of anger, humil-
ity, impatience, escaped from his breast. His mind lit
again upon Rocco's letter and the meeting it instructed
him to attend that night. "My messenger will speak to
you of a simple plan," Rocco had written. "I need you
now. I wish I could be there to discuss this with you, as
in the old days. But we will toast your success side
by side. Listen to this man with the two of your ears,
Natale . . ."

There was someone at the door.

"Good mornin' to y', Nat."

"No top of the morning, Sweeney? Let me hear you
say it, just one time."

"Go on, you silly wop. How are you, Nat? Business
pretty good?"

"Can't complain, Sweeney, and you? Will you take a
cup of coffee?"

"Not for me, Nat. Much too strong for me in the
morning. But now if you had a thimbleful of that
home-made wine, I might drink to your health."

Natale took the half-empty gallon from the sideboard and poured four fingers into a glass.

"Here's to y'," Sweeney said, and drank it down like
a shot of whiskey.

"A salute," Natale said. He pushed the envelopes

with the money forward on the table. He watched the cop undo the silver button below his badge.

"I better be running along, Nat," Sweeney said. He pocketed the marked envelope and put the other one against the celluloid liner of his cap. "Take care, Nat." He wiped his mouth with the back of his big red-haired hand.

"Goodbye, Sweeney."

"Now what is this magic dream that will fix your bones?" he asked the barber.

"Take out your book, Natale, and write me this number. Carefully. One . . . three . . . zero." The barber leaned across the arm of his chair to be certain he had been understood. "One . . . three . . . zero," he repeated. "Fifty cents."

Natale smiled and wrote the number. "And the dream that goes with it?"

The barber rested his neat hand on Natale's sleeve. "Do me no favors," he said.

"Go on, truly would I like to hear it."

The barber went to the cash register. He rang up NO SALE, and took a half-dollar piece from the till. "Natale, I dreamed the Almighty Father was sitting there, where you just sat down."

The collector rose quickly in the chair, and turned sharply around, as though expecting to come face to face with the spirit of God. "One," he said. "And then?"

"He asked to be shaved. When I had finished, he thanked me and left."

"Without paying?"

"Go to the devil! A little after that, he came back.

34

With two others this time," the barber said. He spoke quietly, his eyes closed as though his dream passed before him once again.

"The Holy Trinity," Natale said. He helped himself to the bottle of Eduard Pinaud on the marble shelf and patted the lavender water on his brow. "Three, in any case."

The barber nodded.

"And the zero?"

"When I woke up, they were all gone." The barber opened his eyes. "This I take to signify zero."

Natale shrugged his shoulders. "Just as you say. A fifty-cent piece on one, three, zero."

He collected a bet from each of the cartmen by the curb, and seven more from people who stopped him as he walked down Grand Street to Berto's grocery.

In the crowded shop, from schoolboys buying sandwiches and women bread for dinner, he took another dozen, though Berto himself—an assistant collector—stood behind the counter and could easily have taken the coins as he tallied up.

"Two hunchbacks this morning, Don Natale, in a single hour. That they bring me fortune."

"The month and the day of San Gennaro, Nat, nine ... one ... nine."

The schoolboys bet combinations of yesterday's Yankee score.

And then the store was empty.

"How does it go, Berto?"

"Without pain," the grocer said. He sliced a piece of prosciutto and, nodding toward the tray of dried black olives, gave it to Natale on a piece of bread. "Have you seen the newspaper today?"

35

"Of Tivoli?"

The grocer smiled and nodded. "Light the same afternoon. And they say miracles do not happen." He went to the cash register and withdrew a strip of paper on which he had written the week's bets. "You add it, Natale," he said, and handed over the paper and a pencil from behind his ear.

The collector refused the pencil and folded the paper away. "It is time for lunch, brother. We will settle another time."

His next stop was for two hours, at Cafe Mario. He had a small bottle of wine along with a plate of spaghetti and a piece of veal. When he had eaten, he struck a wooden match for his afternoon de Nobili, and waved to Mario through the half door to the kitchen.

"Light in Tivoli. And it is said a fountain has been constructed in the piazza of Masinalto, my own village." Natale accepted these accomplishments as he had never accepted the miracles of the Church—water to wine, sight to the blind—yet which were more wondrous? Fifteen years ago, he would have bet on champagne spewing from Vesuvius rather than water running in the piazza at Masinalto.

He puffed his cigar, and as the smoke rose about his head, recalled old men like gray figurines of wax placed about the tables in the square. "But for the help of Rocco, I too might have melted in that sun."

And now Rocco's letter in his pocket was like a wall that held two truths apart in his mind: though he had escaped from that death in life, he had accomplished nothing of significance in the new country; though he was well regarded by the other immigrants, he was indeed nothing more than another greenhorn in Little Italy.

"But Rocco was always special," Natale said to himself, "even when he broke his balls working with pick and shovel in the mountains of Oregon." He remembered the story Rocco had told of 1913, when the Wobblies had struck the railroad. He—Rocco—and a handful of others had earned nearly double the track-laying pay by cracking, rather than stones, the square heads of strikers. And when the strike was settled, the men fired and discarded, the Company had made him section boss, and told him to form his own crew of cheapest labor, half the difference of money sought and money paid to be pocketed by himself.

A second-in-command he needed then. In Masinalto, dry village of his birth, waited the boyhood companion for this call. "Come to me now, Natale," Rocco had written twenty-three years before. "The Company pays the passage." Son of a cobbler in a province of poverty where only the rich wore shoes: to Mulberry Street and then to the railroad siding where the crew lived close in a converted freight car stacked with triple bunks for diggers and a single bed for Rocco the boss.

The cigar in Natale's mouth had died out. He rekindled it with the leaping flame of a second match, remembering, far inside the mountain tunnel, the explosion a few months after his arrival at the camp, the field office unattended and the payroll safe a banquet table before Rocco's hungry nimble fingers. Who knows where he had learned that art?

They came back to New York together and put two of the three thousand dollars into a wholesale grocery operation. The remaining thousand they spent on clothes, women, and wine.

And then the war came. Natale thought of the tons of food tenement beds concealed those years: cases and cases of plum tomatoes, dried beans in fifty-pound sacks, gallon tins of olive oil, salt, sugar, pepper—whatever would not rot was bought at any price and hoarded in terror of a return to days of hunger. Just a small per cent of one week's take had been enough to eliminate all but a single visit to the draft center on Broadway. And by the time the war was over, Rocco's pockets were heavy with over two hundred thousand dollars. *Cash.*

He bought surplus Army trucks. He bought warehouses and bodyguards, and as Prohibition flourished, he bought out competition.

He contributed $30,000 to Mussolini's headquarters in Milan, paid for a new school building in Florence, donated $10,000 for the maintenance of St. Peter's, and got a private audience with Pope Pius XI. He turned a nephew in Masinalto into a surgeon in Bologna, immigrant sons of old-time acquaintances into well-paid assistants who sent money to the other side.

Rocco Gargatto was somebody.

In the months July to November 1928, he was shot at four times.

That Christmas morning, Natale, by then Rocco's titular secretary and closest friend, encouraged by his private bank account and frightened by the improving marksmanship of rival gunmen, was granted permission to retire from the Organization. He invested his money legally in corporate bonds and preferred stock on the advice of a broker named Thompson, and the following October was as broke as the day he first had set foot in Rocco's paradise.

Two years later, when it had become obvious total monopoly of bootleg activities in New York was out of the question, Rocco began to diversify his interests. His brothels were soon to him what racing stables were to more legitimate industrialists: a rich man's hobby that more than paid for itself. His fillies were quartered from the Bowery to the Bronx, from Riverside Drive to Sutton Place. A newspaper reporter once observed that to the cognoscenti of every class, Rocco's whorehouses were like a string of Christmas tree lights that circled the city in the gloom of national depression.

Late one afternoon, in Persian-trimmed coat and excellent spirits, Rocco had set out uptown on an inventorial tour that was to combine business with pleasure. He never got north of Fifty-seventh Street. Directly across from Carnegie Hall, a melon-breasted blonde, nineteen years in the sun—Natale closed his eyes and shook his head slowly from side to side—and with the enthusiasm of a three-year-old racing for the big purse, put an end to Rocco's trip. Rocco called for his car, wrapped his coat around his prize, and took her home for keeps.

Madame Butterfly, so Rocco called her, was to earn her keep by providing leads on new talent. Four months later, she accompanied her master on safari into West Virginia. They got as far as the outskirts of Jersey City. An FBI officer at a roadblock there took them into custody and returned them to New York, where Rocco was charged with violation of the Mann Act. The whore signed the complaint, testified against Rocco, joined her boyfriend in Philadelphia, and Rocco went to jail for the first and only time in his life.

Three weeks after his release (he served four months of the two-year sentence), Madame Butterfly, almost twenty and completely naked, was tumbled out of a slow-moving car into a bank of snow before the Centre Street Courthouse, her severed tongue stuck up between her thighs.

Two and a half hours later, Rocco sipped champagne

in a first-class suite aboard the flagship of the Italian line, two hours out of New York, destination Naples.

Natale poured himself the rest of his wine.

Six years of silence, and now the letter.

Mario came from the kitchen, rolling his sleeves down from the elbow, and stopped at Natale's table. "Was the veal to your satisfaction, Natale?"

"Mario, prepared by you, how could it have been less than perfect?"

"I find your compliment even beneath the sarcasm." Mario smiled and touched his friend's shoulder. "A little more wine?"

"Enough," Natale said. He covered the mouth of his glass with his palm. "Thank you. I have accounts to settle before dinner."

At four o'clock he returned to the Lodge and sat again with another coffee. The papers collected that day before him, he made his sums and entered them on the dated page of his notebook. He subtracted the seven dollars paid to Sweeney and drew a double line beneath the balance. Sixty per cent of it, minus pay for his assistant collectors, was his to keep.

So much for the day's work. Natale stood up and stretched his arms above his head, his mouth open wide in a hollow anxious yawn. He looked at the clock on the wall. Time to get going. He reached into each pocket to be sure he carried no books, no bits of numbered paper should they decide to search him. "The letter. They know his name as well as they know Lucifer's." He put Rocco's letter, along with most of his money and the notebook, into the table drawer.

Clean, he walked to Canal Street and headed toward Centre.

Policemen and detectives like shuffling gamblers along the bathroom-tiled hall that stank of disinfectant, a knot of newspapermen covering an arrest, lawyers with briefcases: he hurried by them all and turned into Room 211. The uniformed clerk looked up.

"The Sergeant is not here?"

"He'll be back in a minute," the clerk said.

Natale sat down on the varnished bench by the door. A tall man leaned against the counter and wrote on a small pad of paper. "Another collector," Natale said to himself and laughed aloud. The tall man looked up from his work, gazed away for two puffs of his cigarette, and then turned back to his writing.

Natale lit a de Nobili.

"Put that stinking thing out," the clerk said. "You oughta know by now there's no smoking in here."

The man who wrote turned around and looked at Natale.

"You hear me?" the clerk said.

The Sergeant came in, carrying papers, and said hello to the big writer as he passed him to go behind the counter. The Sergeant sat down at his high desk and opened a thick looseleaf book.

Natale stepped up to the railing.

"You still in the grocery business?" the Sergeant asked.

"Si signore," Natale said. The cigar was in his mouth, unlit.

"No more numbers, eh?" The Sergeant shook his head and made a mark in his book. "Any trouble since the last time?"

"No," Natale said.

The tall man pushed himself away from the counter

and stepped on his cigarette. "Anything else you can tell me?" he asked the clerk.

"That's all I can tell you, Sean. That's all I know."

"I appreciate your help. I better get back to the office. S'long."

"Make sure you spell his name right, Sean," the Sergeant said, and the clerk and the big writer laughed.

The Sergeant made five more marks down a column of the page and closed the book. "You got friends on the Parole Board or something?" he asked Natale.

"Friends on the Parole Board?"

"Yeah. You don't have to come in anymore. And you with still another seven months on the books. Go on, get out of here. I don't want to see your wop face again."

Natale shrugged his shoulders and turned away. He stopped at the door. He lit his cigar and puffed on it till his head was enveloped in the heavy white smoke. Then he dropped the spent match on the floor and smiled at the clerk. He walked out of Room 211, curious about his release from parole and the weekly visits to the office, and grateful for it.


"When we are millionaires we will have fish that tastes of meat. For now, eat what is before you. Quickly," ordered Zia Emilia.

"Pretend it is chicken," said Natale and he winked at his son.

Pietro made a face.

"A fine education you give him," Emilia said sarcastically.

"And what is there of wrong in pretending he has before him something to his taste rather than something that displeases him? As long as he eats the fish though, eh Pietro?" Natale brought his fork to his mouth.

"Beautiful philosophy. The broccoli becomes macaroni, the fish chicken, and the father a hero."

"Eat your chicken, Pietro."

Zia Emilia sighed as the boy ate. "Sainted brother mine," she muttered but she could not conceal her smile.

Natale poured wine for himself and for his son. The boy filled the rest of his glass with water. "To San Gennaro," Natale said, and Pietro touched his glass to his father's.

"A salute," Emilia said, though she herself did not drink.

"And the studies, how do they go?"

Pietro made his face.

Natale held the great round loaf of bread to his chest and sawed off a slice.

"Pretend your studies are . . ." began Zia Emilia.

"Enough," said Natale. He broke the slice of bread in three and put the pieces in the center of the table. "What brings you trouble?"

Pietro shrugged his shoulders and drank his watered wine.

"Have there been more fights?"

"No, Pa."

"Then where is the problem? Geography? History?"

Zia Emilia put down her fork. "Holiest Virgin Mary. What geography? What history? Now he begins his second year."

"Reading, Pa."

"Ah, still the reading."

No one said another word till they had finished eating.

"Now help your aunt in the kitchen, son of mine," Natale said to the boy, "and we will go to the Festa."

Natale sat in the parlor, shadowed by light from the street, and listened to the clatter of the dishes being washed. He undid the buttons of his vest. His thoughts hurried back to Rocco. "Whatever it is that is needed of me," Natale silently swore, "I give it with all my strength and all my soul. God knows my heart bursts with desire to do."

His son, suddenly touching his knee, scattered his reverie and brought the boy's problems of school back to his mind. "Pietro Pietro Pietro," Natale said softly and lifted him to his knee.

"Do we not go to the Festa?"

Natale smiled. "Still an hour must pass before the Mass begins," he said. "Listen. You must study well your lessons, am I understood?"

The boy nodded.

"What is your name?" Natale asked in English.

"My name is Pietro Sbagliato. Capital P-i-e-t-r-o, capital S-b-a-g-l-i-a-t-o."

"Bravo." Natale put down his cigar. He joined his hands before him and wiggled his thumbs in such a way that light from the lamp at his side projected an animal's head onto the wall.

"A rabbit. R-a-b-i-t."

"And this?"

"A cat. C-a-t."

"And this?"

"D-o-g."

"Bravo Pietro." Natale kissed the boy's brow.

"What is the hour?"

"Whey. Be patient," Natale said. "There is still time."

44

Pietro nodded. "Time for a story?"

Natale smiled, drew a deep breath, and leaned back in his chair. Pietro leaned back too, and settled his head on his father's chest. They closed their eyes.

For all the times it had been told, the fairy tale had become truth now, and the house in Masinalto it described more real than the kitchen they had just left.

It stood alone in a country where mountains rose many times taller than the tallest buildings, where grapes grew big as plums in vineyards like giant steps to the sea below, where rain fell only at night so as not to destroy a single day of sunshine.

There were many many rooms in the house, more rooms than could be imagined, for the house had been built at a time when entire families used to travel from far away and spend weeks and weeks in visits. When Pappa was a boy, he used to play in the second and third story of that house and explore those unused rooms with friends as though they were chambers in a castle.

The floors were made of stone polished till it shone like marble, and red velvet draperies hung from the ceiling above the windows like the stage curtain in the Endicott Theatre. From the balconies outside those windows, one could look down at the avenue below and wave to the ladies and gentlemen passing by in carriages drawn by black and white horses.

Don Natale continued the story. He told of winemakers, their legs stained purple to the knee, feet scrubbed with heavy brushes before they went working, singing and grasping the great knotted rope from above as they danced the wine from the grapes. He told of himself driving a donkey cart with cavernous barrels to Salerno, and of the time bandits stopped him on the way and filled their goatskins with Sbagliato wine before letting him go

45

on. He told of a sudden mysterious frost that destroyed the vineyards and the family wealth as quickly and surely as if each vine itself had been pulled by the roots, and he told of the poverty that fell upon them like a dust storm.

He told of Rocco Gargatto, already in America, a power even then, building the railroad through the faraway forest and mountains of Oregon.

Natale opened his eyes. "You will learn of this railroad in your lessons one day," he said, "and perhaps they will not say Italians built it. But you will know.

"When Rocco learned of the disaster of the vineyards, he sent for me to work on the railroad. He paid for the steamship passage that lasted sixteen days across the ocean.

"In one year I would have enough to call Granma and Granpa and Zia Emilia to me in America. Perhaps Emilia would marry a rich American. God knows what we imagined in those days.

"The first night in this country I slept in the rooms of a friend of Rocco. You know where the barbershop of Luigi stands now?"

Pietro nodded.

"Upstairs from the barbershop, in a bed alive with bugs, I cried for the beauty behind me. But so was Oregon beautiful, working with pick to move mountains for the railroad, beneath a sky clear like the eyes of the Holy Virgin, like the sky of my country. After dark, at night, we used to go to the sidecars where we lived, five peasants seven thousand miles from family. But we knew the same people in the old country, and after eating—and one ate well, too, for the cook was one of us after all, and it was Rocco who ordered food for every section of the

46

line—we talked and sounded the mandolin and sang. I was lucky to have such a job. The towns were thick with men looking for work.

"One day, far inside the mountain in a tunnel we had dug, an explosion shattered the soul of the earth and sealed us alone with God. Entombed six hours, I swore on the head of my mother if ever I saw daylight I would never fight the mountain again.

"Rocco was with the ones who rescued us. Twenty-seven Christians were buried alive that day. It has never come known how the explosion took place. The newspapers said it was the Communists, others said it was men desperate for work hoping for the places that would be left vacant by the dead.

"The next day we took our savings and came again to New York.

"Again it was Rocco who fed me. With all he had learned of the grocery business as steward of the railroad and with all his friends in the Old Country, he became an importer. And he made me his agent, though I was ready to work as a digger of ditches.

"Now I dressed like a prince, with spats and patent leather shoes like Jimmy Walker and a vest of brocaded silk. Yet who could speak a word of English? My customers were brothers, and that is how we made it, one hand washing the other. I took their orders and for their money got them salami, capocollo, formaggio Locatelli, olio d'oliva, prosciutto e fave seche.

"And we began to make a little wine for steady customers, for none could be had for the love of God.

"Rocco and I got rich. Not rich *really* rich like Rocco before he left, but what was there we did not have? And every month, the sack of money I sent home.

"From one family to the next, I found your mother."

Natale crossed himself, his son in his arms. "But how beautiful she was, with hair like the daughter of Emanuel the King."

From the kitchen, the sound of cupboard doors slamming had ceased and Zia Emilia was embroidering at her frame.

"With hair like the daughter of the King and the beauty of a saint. Her father was overcome by my proposal of marriage on my second sight of her, she one of seven sisters and those times hard. It was like buying a sack of flour, and that is the enthusiasm she had for me. It was no good: a doctor, a lawyer, an educated prince she had dreamed of, not a rich one. And for all the love I gave her, and consideration, never a vulgar word.

"You brought her life as much as she brought you yours, son of mine. She put away her dreams in you as surely as she gave you her breast, and then she died."

The story was over. Natale opened his eyes and kissed his son gently on the cheek.

From where he sat, he could see, through the doorway of his bedroom, the photograph of his wife in the tortoise-shell frame. She was seventeen, two years before marriage, in a white dress with puff sleeves, her wavy hair fading now into the sepia background. Yet the fragile cheekbones, like blue-white china, still shone in the picture.

The boy slid down from his lap. "Pappa, see how it is dark outside," he said hesitantly.

Natale caressed the boy's face roughly. "Run. Take a sweater and we will go to the Festa." Pietro gone, he took his watch from his vest pocket: still an hour and a half remained.

48

Emilia, with tight mouth, glanced at him as he entered the kitchen. "Have you finished filling him with unworthiness?"

"Do you want coffee?" Natale asked quietly, as though she had not spoken.

"I have taken it."

"Then let me take mine in peace." Still his voice was low.

"Rocco here, Rocco there. Why do you tell him of such a man?" Emilia threw off her glasses and they bounced from the framed pillowcase onto the floor. Natale picked them up and offered them to her. She waved them aside and hunted in her basket for cotton of the color she needed. "Answer me. Why give him such a hero, such an animal for admiration?"

"Too much now," Natale shouted. He threw open his hands before him as though to release in her face Rocco's credentials. "Knighted Cavaliere by Mussolini in Rome. Blessed in private audience by the Holy Father. Donated God knows how many thousands for the sake of Italianita. What more do you demand of a man? Please, Emilia," he said, "you know nothing about him. Only the trash you once read in the paper. If you know how he helped us, time after time."

"Jesus Christ helped us too. Why do you not tell the boy of that Savior?"

"And you speak of blasphemy," Natale said in sudden softness. "Listen to yourself. And in that moment of peace, I will take my coffee."

They fell silent, Emilia's needle like a hornet leaving its mark in red as it zipped again and again through the linen.

Pietro came in. "Pronto, Pappa," he said. "Let's go."

Natale rinsed his cup and left it in the sink. He dried his hands and went to the window box and picked a fresh flower. And picked another for the button-hole of his boy who smiled and took his father's hand.

"We see one another," Natale said to Emilia. She nodded, continued with her work.

In the Church of the Most Precious Blood they heard Mass, all the vestry's candelabra like golden sparklers flanking Father Carrino as the old priest held high the chalice in white hands. Natale prayed that Rocco's request of him was great and noble and that he, Natale, would accommodate it gloriously. At his side, Pietro prayed for a red balloon.

They watched Father Carrino walk slowly to the senior squad of altar boys beyond the rail, and lead them to the niche near the rear of the church where the plaster statue of San Gennaro, decked with greenhouse gladioluses, waited to be carried through the streets. To Father Carrino's whispered admonitions of care—he could be heard on the opposite wall—the strong anxious arms lowered the saint from his perch and placed him on the dolly, the one ordinarily used at Requiem Mass.

Benediction's censer laying smoke of grace before him, the fat priest, like a float himself, led the procession to the street and supervised San Gennaro's transfer to the chassis that waited at the curb. The two tallest altar boys, their candles' flames fanned by the outdoor breeze, climbed aboard the float and quickly fastened a dozen ribbons to the ring of flowers. Father Carrino blessed the crowd. The procession moved on, Natale and the boy following alongside, joined at every corner by scores of devotees who pinned dollar bills to San Gennaro's trailing ribbons while policemen doffed their caps and held up cross-street traffic.

At last they stopped in silence just opposite the bandstand in the middle of Mulberry Street. At a signal from the priest, Maestro Martini raised and suddenly brought down his baton. Cornets and violins introduced the Grand March from *Aïda*. A switch was thrown, and the night was bright.

A gentle tug on Natale's sleeve: "Pappa, could I have a lemon ice?"

"No ice, son of mine. It freezes the stomach. Ice cream if you want it."

Pietro nodded. They walked past the clickety-clack of the gambling wheel to the ice cream tent. Natale bought him a dixie cup and, without being asked, a red Mickey Mouse balloon on a long string, which he fastened to the boy's velvet belt. Then they strolled down the middle of the street, Pietro gazing at the red balloon high above his head.

They stopped to watch the tarantella danced to an accordian and guitar, the musicians seated on folding chairs in the doorway of a store. The dancers, laughing and breathless, clapped their hands, turning and spinning, the plaited skirt of an American girl swirling from her hips and showing her long, fine legs. Faster and faster till the music passed the dancers. And then they stopped, perspiring and dizzy, and Natale watched the blonde one take the arm of her necktied boy as the crowd absorbed them like a sponge. "How they love us," he said in Italian to the guitarist, "this time of year," and father and son continued through the scene.

Natale took out his watch and saw its face in the

candlelight of San Gennaro. It was time to leave. He glanced through the rows of wooden chairs before the statue of the saint. "Look, there is Zia Emilia in the front row on the end," he said to Pietro. "Stay with her now and I will kiss you goodnight in your bed." He watched as the boy went to his aunt and she set him in her lap. Her companions looked up at his arrival and then continued praying as they stared at his high balloon. Natale waved to his sister, and hurried away.

Morrone's place was on the next street, and the sidewalk before it was without illumination; the Committee on Lights had not asked the undertaker for a contribution, nor had he volunteered one. The only light in his window was the lavender clock that indicated nine-fifteen as Natale went to it through the trumpet solo and the laughter of the night at his back.

The blind on the door was drawn, but knowledge that Rocco's own envoy was waiting gave him courage to enter. In the dark he recognized the scent of mourning roses and carnations and the soul of candles spent. Instinctively he crossed himself as he closed the door behind him. The glow from the window showed a potted palm across the threadbare carpet and suggested folding chairs along the opposite wall. In that corner, hidden from the street by heavy drapes and a barren bier, was the bright outline of the door to Morrone's office. He went to it and knocked gently. A pause. He was about to knock again when the undertaker from within called "Enter." Don Natale opened the door.

# CHAPTER 4

"ON THE POINT OF NINE-FIFTEEN," the undertaker said, reaching out with two hands to draw Don Natale into the room. Perfumes of the chapel crept in on the collector's coat. "Colonel Tedesco, this is the one. Don Natale, Colonel Tedesco, aide to Prince Ralli and special ambassador of Il Duce's Imperial Government to this country."

"I am honored, Colonel," Natale said. He bowed. "Please do not discomfort yourself on my account," he said as Tedesco rose out of his chair at the introduction.

"How could I present you with Rocco's regards with my bottom resting on silk brocade?" Tedesco said with a laugh. "It is I who am honored, Don Natale. Your friend Rocco in Rome speaks exceedingly well of you. You will take a little liqueur with us? Morrone, a glass for the collector." With a hand on the collector's shoulder, Tedesco led Natale to the chair beside his own. "I was about to tell Signor Morrone a story," he said. "Your knock on the door was perfectly timed, and saves me the trouble of repetition."

The undertaker handed Natale a strega, and refilled the other two glasses.

"Tell me, Don Natale," Tedesco began, "do you remember an animal called Guido Sempione?"

Natale looked at him quickly. "The Communist? The one who writes that workers' rag, the strike leader who is the disgrace of every honest Italian in this country?"

Tedesco smiled. "You have placed him." He touched the glass of sweet burning liqueur to his lips. "Now let me give you good news. Sempione will be dead before morning."

Quickly he raised his hand to stifle questions. "Later, my friends. Listen to me for now. Sempione's death is a Fascist necessity, ordered by Mussolini himself, in part to end the front-page editorials written by the pig that insult the dignity and benevolence of the Premier. And in part because of Sempione's statements concerning the recognition by America of Abyssinia as an Italian state."

Tedesco smiled at Natale. "Now, in America, the execution of assignments such as these is the responsibility of your friend Rocco Gargatto. His contacts here are superb. In this Sempione affair, Rocco also has the pleasure of ridding himself of a personal toothache.

"Forgive me, Collector, if I take a moment to explain to Signor Morrone something you already know." Without awaiting a reply, Tedesco turned to the undertaker.

"Not many years ago, my dear Morrone, it was quite common for enemies of Il Duce to choose exile in America over a Fascist prison. Most often, their entry into this country was illegal, without benefit of passports, et cetera.

"This was in the year Nineteen . . ." He paused, looking at Natale for help. "Nineteen what, Don Natale?" he asked kindly.

The collector turned away. "I do not remember," he said.

54

"The year is unimportant. What *is* important is the fact that Rocco reached every one of these exiles—rich men, all of them—and threatened to expose them to Washington unless they paid his own special immigration fee. The one or two who refused were indeed returned to Italy by the American government and executed by the Black Shirts.

"To get back to Guido Sempione, our Communist editor. It was he who exposed Rocco's unique enterprise. But by so doing, he implicitly admitted knowledge of illegal aliens, and was sentenced to six months in prison for refusing to answer questions as to their whereabouts."

Tedesco glanced amiably at Natale. "You smile now, Don Natale. You remember with what ardor the FBI here pressed for Sempione's conviction, with what joy they took him south to prison, delighted to be free of his harangue six months."

The smile on Natale's face spread, and he nodded. "Nineteen thirty, Colonel. A beautiful victory for Rocco."

"Who knew he could count on your good memory. You do not disappoint him." Tedesco turned to the undertaker. "And now you must excuse us if you feel our conversation seems to exclude you, Signor Morrone. It does not. I urge you to listen carefully."

Tedesco stood up and steadied himself against the table. "We come to the point of Rocco's letter to you, my dear Natale, to the significance of my voyage to America, and to this meeting here tonight." He walked slowly to Natale's side and grasped his shoulder.

"It is you who have been chosen to remove Sempione from this life." Immediately he shook his head and shut his eyes to Natale's incredulous expression. "Not yet, my dear Collector." He poured more strega. "Drink, drink, my friend," he urged, but Natale did not drink.

"Of course, you are surprised. I was surprised, after all. You will hate me when I say I spoke out against Rocco's choice of you, against entrusting an assassination of such magnitude to the hands of a collector. But your friend is a master at this kind of thing, and has prepared an itinerary even a child could follow. I am now convinced, Don Natale," Tedesco said in a low voice, "that you are the man to see this plan through."

He struck a match for his cigarette. "Please, let me finish," he said quickly as the collector cleared his dry throat and tried for speech. "You have everything to gain and nothing to lose. Do you not understand?" he asked softly. "In this way Rocco rewards your friendship, so close for so many years. He understands your true desire to be of service to your country and to elevate yourself in Fascist eyes. At the same time, Rocco understands your desire to return his kindness and consideration of years ago. Guido Sempione provides the perfect opportunity to satisfy, with a single blow, if you will, your two wishes.

"There is no risk, Don Natale," Tedesco said. He smiled, gazing at the collector's fear, the wide eyes, slack jaw, the bloodless pallor about the cheeks. "Certainly you can trust your friend Rocco. There is no risk, Natale," Tedesco repeated, "do you understand that? No risk. Should you be apprehended—totally out of the question, for want of motive—bail will be secretly arranged through the Consulate. Here there is no problem. You see, Sempione sticks in the craw of this country's government too. God knows every factory owner in America will celebrate his end. And the police as well as the FBI will breathe a great sigh of good riddance.

"Everything is in order," Tedesco continued. "A passport, already framed," he took the document from his coat pocket and laid it on the table before them, "would permit first-class passage to the other side." He took out the second passport and held it before Natale's face, the photograph of the boy like a sudden spark of light in a dream of darkness and confusion in the mind of the collector. "Nor have we forgotten your son."

Tedesco walked slowly about the room, his hands clasped behind his back. "Let us continue to assume the worst—that you are found out, that you have been released on the bail arranged through the Consulate, and that you and your son have traveled first-class to the other side." Tedesco leaned low before the still and frightened face of the collector and spread his arms before him. "An additional reward, Don Natale," he said secretly, as though to keep this information from the undertaker who sat across the table ignored, "Commission to the Order of Savoy, and the accompanying allowances—the wealth and privileges accorded to a patriot of Fascist Italy."

He finished his liqueur and filled the glass again, offering none to the others this time. He sat down in his chair and crossed his long legs before him. He waited a while before going on, to let the full import of all he had said sink into the collector's slow mind. Suddenly his heart was stabbed by the icicle of doubt that had formed during his speech to Natale: had Rocco been mistaken indeed in his evaluation of the collector's enthusiasm for action?

He stood up and resumed his attack. "Your son would be with you, your sister in this country never again would think of money. All that, assuming you are forced to leave this country." Tedesco produced the pack of bills the Secretary had given him at the Consulate and tossed them neatly into Natale's lap. "Three thousand dollars if you stay in the United States. Put away, in fifteen years it would insure the medical education of your only son."

Tedesco smiled more broadly now, showing his bright teeth. "Consider closely, Don Natale, before you speak. After all, there is time before your decision must be known."

He turned at last to Morrone the undertaker. "What do you think?" he asked with exaggerated politeness. "Do you not think he would be unreasonable to refuse an offer of this kind?" Tedesco laughed a little bit. "But look at you. You seem more frightened than the collector himself. What a courageous staff we keep in New York."

"It is not a question of courage," the undertaker said unevenly.

Emboldened by another's voice, Natale raised his hands to his breast. "But I am not a gun," he cried. "I have never killed."

Tedesco turned his smile on him. "Do not remind me of that, please. My friend, I did not choose you. Rest assured though, that the man who did, your own Rocco, has complete faith in your enthusiasm, your courage, your ability. Believe me, Collector," Tedesco said honestly, "he would not let you do this thing without trust in your heart and in your safety."

Tedesco stood up and stretched his arms and yawned. "Of course you cannot be forced to take your Rocco's lead. But remember, the very offer of this honor," he said through suddenly tight lips, "involves you inextricably. Rejection would be interpreted in Rome as expression of disloyalty. I do not doubt that such live potential evidence might—I say *might*—of necessity be destroyed to avoid possible embarrassment to the Imperial Government. The next candidate, already selected and schooled, would have not one assignment, but two." He paused. "All is plain between us, Collector?"

Don Natale nodded his head slowly.

Tedesco examined his wristwatch. "It is now exactly ten twenty-two. You have just under two hours in which to convince yourself one way or the other. The decision is yours to make." He moved toward the door, then stopped and turned again to Natale. "On the question of Pietro, your son," he said gently. "Know that from this moment until we see one another here again at twelve and a quarter, he is under the eyes of men with no heart for a young soul. God protect us from any misunderstanding, Collector. For the health of the boy, stay away from him tonight. As I know you will stay a safe distance from the police."

Tedesco took the collector's hand and ushered him to the door of the chapel. "Till later," he said, Don Natale holding his hand without strength, expression gone from his face.


He had waited still and silent before the undertaker's door, for the music and the laughter, the inviting calls of cartmen hawking nougat candy and coffee ice, for the colored lights that spanned the night to work the magic of a lamp snapped on in darkness—to deliver him from the dream of his life.

And then he had gone on like a blindman whose dim eyes would recognize the buoy of a red balloon, his son, through people bunched like dried flowers drifting in the street. Slowly at first, he came to know the nightmare was reality strung on the loom a score and more years before with his passage to this country on Rocco's behest; swiftly then, he saw that the thing made by his hand could be taken apart by his hand, ripped into pieces too small to bind.

"What do I do?" he cried to himself. "I am no killer, I cannot kill. What is this asked of me now? Rocco, Rocco, in the name of Christ, what torment is this you steep me in? How do you drag me to tear at the life I lead for my son? Why do you force my face in the past? Oh leave me, Rocco my heart, leave me alone. If there were some way to reach you, you would excuse me from this assignment of death, I know." The sudden wild thought of a telephone call flashed through his mind like a roman candle and burned out before he could grasp and fully consider it. Across the street, Sweeney the cop drank beer with Father Carrino. Natale turned away from them and into the crowd from fear of spilling his heart, Pietro alone under the eyes of the others.

In a few steps he cried aloud at the balloon he saw at last, floating nearly second-story high: yellow, not the red one of his son. And yet he hurried toward it, telling himself that yellow it had always been; then, that Pietro had exchanged balloons with a friend; then, that the one of red had burst and had been replaced with yellow by Emilia. But it was a girl child who held that long string, her other hand in the hand of her mother.

He went then into a thick ungiving crowd that had fastened itself to the bandstand like mussels to the piles of a pier. When the band began to play, he remembered that San Gennaro and the candles and the chairs had been removed from this place to the other, where Emilia had taken over the boy.

He fought his way through and out of that crowd like a man swimming under water without breath. As he hurried away, someone called his name. "Natale! Don Natale! Here. Look at him!" and they laughed. It was the barber and Mario on the sidewalk of his cafe, waving to him with a great raffia-wrapped bottle of chianti. "A glass of wine! Natale, come drink with us!"

The street was quiet, like a church, around the statue. The old people prayed there still, as before, Pietro with his sweet head against the shoulder of his aunt and the balloon like the world in his lap. Natale wiped the cool perspiration from his brow and felt a long wavering sigh escape from his breast.

He gazed at the boy. Tedesco's warning returned to him. He tried to determine which of the faithful in the folding chairs had been assigned as guard, which of the men would act should he take his son in his arms and run—where? Home? The police? Father Carrino? Escape tonight would be only that; tomorrow they would surely reach him.

Never taking his eyes from Pietro's face, he backed out of the street onto the sidewalk and leaned against the window of a store. He glanced once at the plaster saint and bowing his head, his son still plain before him, made the Sign of the Cross on his breast and kissed the knuckle of his index finger as though he held a crucifix.

"San Gennaro," he prayed, "help me. Free me from this box in which I have sealed myself. Break this bond I myself have forged with hot words and hands of years ago. Never have I killed, Padrone, this you know. Take from my back the prod that presses me close to the ledge of my window." He waited and gazed head on at the painted face of the altar saint. "This I promise, San

Gennaro, you who see to yesterday and tomorrow with heavenly eyes and best understand today: never more will I yearn for greatness above me, never stain again an honest father's life with cravings for station beyond me. Satisfied will I be with father's love fulfilled and dream ahead of boy grown into doctor, pride of old man's end of life. San Gennaro dear to me, having wished upon myself this robe, let me cast it off now, and burn it in my heart."

His eyes closed for an instant and boy and saint blurred out as Natale gave himself utterly to the forgiveness and release he prayed for. Then with a snaking chill he recalled the lie of Rocco's rescue in the cave, having twisted and distorted the actuality of that explosion to fit the image of the hero in a tale told earlier in the night, and all his life. There, in that tale, he had told the boy of an oath sworn, a pact taken with God: that should he ever find himself again in pure air, never would he fight again the mountains of Oregon, never having been trapped in a cave, no pact ever sworn.

Cold memory of that deception, reasonable enough a few hours before, drowned his San Gennaro prayer and left Natale afraid again, and alone.

In the street before him, his sister Emilia huddled his son to her black-skirted thigh and moved him along at her side in the direction of home. Motionless, afraid his fearful heart would betray his watch, Natale waited for the men to rise from the varnished chairs. They did, hats pulled low like the hooded bastards they were, the two of them, one on either side of where the boy and aunt had sat. As they passed, the closer one nodded to him, to let him know they knew he was there. And he watched them go into the music and the light, close to the old woman his sister and his only son.

The swagger was gone: the enthusiasm and antici-
pation of greatness that had accompanied him out of his
house had turned to stone. He walked slowly, dumb, in
the bubbling crowd, the two hours before him a scalding
field he would pass through he knew, to take in his hand
the star he had reached for, the grip of a gun.

Soon he found himself before Cafe Mario, where the
sidewalk was littered with tables and chairs of metal
brought up from the cellar once each year at the time of
San Gennaro. Mario's wife and two sons hurried to customers with sandwiches and wine, pastry and coffee.
Mario himself sat by the doorway now, in starched collar
and high-buttoned coat, and smoked a de Nobili while he
poured from a special half gallon for a select circle of
Sons of Italy and a few immigrant peasants from Paterson. He stood up in his place when he saw Natale at the
edge of the street and called to him, glass in hand.
Arm around his shoulder, Mario introduced him to the
peasants from Paterson as Don Natale the Collector.

"Beautiful wine, Mario," Natale said quietly, tasting
the wine, knowing Mario himself had made it.

"Of five years ago," Mario said. "Only the best for
San Gennaro."

At the table beside them, two peasants and Luigi the
barber talked. "NRA, SEC, CCC," a peasant sang. "Who
knows what it means? But this I know. Now there is
more money and more to eat. Do I speak truth or not?"

"The cripple is a Communist," the barber said. He
held his glass bottom-up to Mario and smiled. "Must I
whistle through my lips to indicate an empty glass?"

The peasant waited till the glass was refilled, as
though unwilling to speak while the barber's attention
was taken by desire for wine. But then he slapped both

hands onto the table and leaned forward. "A Communist?" he demanded.

The barber nodded, looking away, convinced of the truth he spoke. "How else does one explain his refusal to accept Abyssinia as ours? Yet his recognition of the Union Soviet?"

"Look, Luigi," the peasant said. "No one is perfect. Eh? For how does one explain the marriage of Mussolini and the German Hitler?"

Natale sighed and turned away. "What is the matter?" Mario asked him quietly. "You seem half the man to me tonight, Natale."

Natale shut his eyes. "If you knew, Mario," he said, "if only you knew." Even as he spoke, the sepulchral scent of flowers remembered from that hidden room, the danger for his child, the announcement of Rocco's proposal that he, Natale Sbagliato, rid Italy of Guido Sempione, and Tedesco's warning; all of it came together now and permeated his insides like the choking smoke of a damp leaf fire.

"But see how you throw off that perspiration," Mario said. "What disturbance have you?"

Natale smiled and shook his head. He opened his eyes and took a drink of wine.

"You seem to me half drunk," Mario said. "What else have you tasted tonight?"

"A small glass of strega."

Mario threw up his hands and laughed. "Then sleep in your own bed, brother mine."

Natale smiled. The peasant was still talking. "You speak of marriage. Do you know that Il Duce has asked the people to donate their gold wedding rings to bolster the Treasury? Do you know that?" the peasant asked.

64

"There is a great shortage of gold," Luigi the barber said. "In place of the gold, donors receive rings of iron which serve the original purpose of the wedding band."

"And I suppose the ardent Fascist considers his iron ring symbol of the great mystic union between the Italian nation and its God, eh?" the peasant asked. "Like the single ring of a nun and her marriage to Christ, I suppose that is what he feels. I hope, for the benefit of us all," the peasant said—he banged his heavy glass against the table—"those rings never become the links of a chain."

"Enough," cried Mario full voice. "Upstairs, everyone, to see the Little Flower bloom."

"Is it true the Mayor is to speak?"

"So it has been promised. Don Natale, do you come or must I carry you in my arms?"

Natale drained his glass and was about to stand to follow Mario when a name another peasant spoke hammered at his heart: "Guido Sempione . . ."

The one to be killed.

". . . nor is he a Communist, brother mine."

"Whey, enough," Mario shouted. "Do not forget the significance of this night. Enough politics, for the love of Christ."

"No no no no, Mario," Luigi insisted. "We speak not of politics but in terms of patriotism. For was it not Communism that destroyed our country before Mussolini put it down?"

The peasant sighed. "On just this ignorance has he built his prison empire. Communism in Italy was already beneath six feet of earth and stone when your Duce came to power."

They rose and walked behind Mario in a line through

the restaurant. Natale followed them, unable to break away now. Only with restraint did he keep from cracking the ignorant peasant with news of Sempione's impending death. His secret knowledge suddenly raised him high above them in his mind, and he felt he occupied a private box from which he could direct the course of history.

They passed through the noisy kitchen where Mario's wife sliced prosciutto with a foot-long blade. Mario took three bottles of wine and the party followed him up the cool pantry-scented stairway to the first floor front. They went to the windows and stumbled out onto the fire escape.

Mario took his corkscrew from his pocket and pulled open two bottles and passed them around to his guests as they settled on window sills and on the iron steps. The arches of light reached up and colored their faces red and green. "We look like so many Italian flags," somebody said.

"Look, Luigi," the peasant began again, gently, "Sempione is not a Communist . . ."

Natale squeezed his eyes shut and pressed his hands to his forehead. His skin was dripping.

"Communist, jailbird, troublemaker—*that* is your Guido Sempione," Luigi insisted. "Someone pass me a drop of wine before I die of thirst."

"He is not a Communist," the peasant said again. "He was a Socialist though," he added with a grin. "In fact, he was forced to leave his village in province Abruzzi for political reasons. Just like Il Duce, incidentally. Both of them were Socialists if you like that better."

The barber filled his throat with Mario's wine. Below, the band rested and in the nearly quiet street, children fought sleep as they waited for the firework finale of the first night of the Festa.

The peasant took the bottle from Luigi when the barber was through with it and drank from it fully. Then he wiped his red mouth in the palm of his hand. "Sempione goes where trouble already exists and cultivates it—gives it strength and character—and nurses it along. He is like a gardener who finds a common weed and miraculously transforms it into a rare and beautiful blossom."

"You would have us believe the instigation of strikes and riots is the cultivation of beauty?" Luigi looked desperately for support at Mario and the other peasants and at Natale, who said nothing.

"In a sense, absolutely," the peasant said quietly. "Without Sempione, these little troubles might have been ignored. Sempione develops them into fine catastrophes that approach the dimension of a national crisis. For only then are the workers heard."

Mario opened another bottle of old wine. "Have you finished now, you two?"

"This one knows not of what . . ." Luigi started angrily.

"Whey," Mario cried, "are you going to let us hear the introduction of Mayor LaGuardia or not?"

Their silence came in time for Maestro Martini's introduction, not of Mayor LaGuardia but of Michele Volpo, and Mario sighed and said," "More politics, whether I like it or not. Michele Volpo, the King of Pinball."

There was little applause for Volpo in the street. Nevertheless he threw up his arms as if trying to quiet a thunderous ovation. Finally he took hold of the microphone. "Friends of Italy," he called out, "I bring you the personal regards and salutations of the Honorable Fiorello LaGuardia."

"In other words the Mayor will not be with us this evening," Mario said. "Nor does he know this pig takes his name."

"You know what I stand for as well as you know your mothers," Volpo yelled. "I stand for the recognition of the Italian people as American citizens—American citizens with the full rights to work and live as human beings. Because I know what it is to say goodbye to the house of your birth."

His voice crossed the street full and clear like a dramatic tenor of the Metropolitan, passed into Natale's head, and left there a residue of sadness and joy that sifted to the collector's heart.

"I know what it is to cross the ocean in a ship unworthy of beasts of burden. I know what it is to land in a strange country, expecting trees of gold along the streets, only to find the trees grow the thorns of the crown of Christ. I know the agony of words malpronounced and improperly used, the laughter and the scorn of ignorants heaped upon you like shovels of earth on a living grave. I know the pain and demoralization of the second-rate citizenship imposed by the ruling classes. I know these things, I swear to you I know them, here, in my heart, for I have lived your lives and dried away your tears."

Below, on the sidewalk, an old man lifted a child high onto his shoulders to see "the president."

"We, progeny of the She-Wolf, huddled together in rotting buildings like ten thousand sheep in a storm. Our history burns with the names of Michelangelo, Leonardo, Galileo, Marconi, Caruso—who here could not name

68

twenty others? And yet we stood by and gnashed our teeth in impotent desperation as they sent to their innocent death a fish peddler and a maker of shoes. We neither spoke their language nor knew their laws, and helpless were we in our ignorance."

The crowd mourned.

"But a new life was born for us through Salvatore Catanzaro, the first Italian assemblyman, and our own Mayor of New York, Fiorello LaGuardia."

They came alive. They shouted and whistled and waved Italian flags that appeared from nowhere and suddenly sped through their ranks.

"Help me," Volpo yelled to the microphone, his arms high over his head. "Help me as you helped Catanzaro and LaGuardia, and let me help you as they have helped you. Help me bring you steady work."

"Eviva!"

"Help me bring you schools for your children."

"Eviva!"

"Help me bring you dignity."

"Eviva!"

"Help me . . ."

"GOD HELP US." A broken-English cry ripped Volpo's plea and seemed to pin him to the evening sky. "God help *us*." That cry scattered the crowd and it backed away, caught unaware, frightened by the force. "God help us if the kind of talk that gangster throws sticks in the eyes around him." A city wastebasket was suddenly overturned and the man with the voice leaped up on it and grabbed hold of the lamppost for support. "What has he said to you?" he demanded of the faces turned up around him. "What has he said to you that you have not known all your lives?"

Luigi the barber, standing and pointing down straight-armed as with a sword at the man shouting in the street below, cried, "There. There is your Sempione. Not a troublemaker, eh? And then what do you call him?" he demanded of the peasant.

The peasant smiled. "He is beautiful. Saint Peter himself would learn blasphemy in company of the devil."

From the fire escape, Natale saw him: an old man, angry.

"Not one goddamn word about ability. Not one goddamn word about a plan. He talks to you of Michelangelo as though salvation waited in the past."

Natale saw him plainly. A big-boned old man with the rimless glasses of a country doctor. The beard of anarchy spreading from bright full cheeks. A wide-brimmed, cream-colored felt hat like a cowboy in the American films. A great black scarf tied loosely at his neck, waving like a flag as he cursed Volpo, his racketeer backers, his motives for seeking office.

Suddenly a giant with red hair broke into the open ring. The old man glanced down, then looked away and clenched his fists. "Politics is a business with them. It makes them rich. Once they are elected they are paid to shut their eyes to the crimes that deprive the poor. Like police breakups of picket lines. They stall minimum wage legislation till you will die at your machines, brothers, before..."

The red-headed giant grabbed Sempione's legs. "Get down," he ordered.

". . . before racketeers like Volpo will fight for the forty-hour week for the benefit of you and others like you."

The giant set his shoulder against Sempione's legs,

wrapped his arms around the steady knees, and suddenly pushed with all his force.

Sempione fell face downward to the sidewalk, like a toppled statue, unbending.

Natale crushed his eyes shut and inaudibly prayed the old man had been killed. He considered Tedesco as he prayed, and whether Sempione's death by falling would satisfy him and so release Pietro from the guard of the men who watched him, and redeem himself, Natale, from the honor to which he had been made obligated with his life. "That he is dead, my God, that he has been killed." Afraid, he opened his eyes.

The crowd backed away from the tumbling waste-basket that had crashed beneath Sempione's fall as the old man slowly rose to his knees and searched the ground around him with a bloody hand for the glasses that lay smashed in the street. When he turned, Natale saw his face was bruised and his lip split cleanly as though it had been cleft with an axe; but that was all.

"I told you to get down, old sonofabitch," the giant yelled. His voice trembled. "Go home now. Go fix your face. Your speech is uninvited."

Sweeney the cop was nowhere.

Sempione got up. "This is America," he said, kindly. "Everyone can speak his mind here. But you, you would not understand this, Fascist bastard." He righted the wastebasket, and as he climbed back up, denouncing the blackguard attack on his right of free speech, two police-men smashed through the crowd. With three silent blows of their nightsticks, they knocked him down from his place. Then they backed a van to where he lay and pushed Sempione through its narrow gate like street cleaners hauling away a mattress.

As the truck drove off, Maestro Martini waved all his seventeen pieces into a discordant Grand March.

The next best thing had happened: Guido Sempione was in custody of the police; his arrest spelled liberation for Natale.

"Bastards," the peasant screamed after the truck, "Fascist bastards. They crucify another Christ and we let them take him without a word."

"He escaped lightly tonight," Luigi the barber said quietly. "Some of the beatings he has taken, the Communist son of a bleeding whore."

Natale stood up. "They have saved his life," he murmured to the peasant, "believe me." He touched the man on the shoulder. "And I have no love for him."

The great weight was off his chest. No decision waited like a guillotine before him. Joy, warm like a bath, flooded through him and washed away his fears, his hatred, his desire. Pietro would be returned. Tomorrow would be like yesterday.

Mario took hold of Natale's sleeve. "And where do you go now? The artificial fires begin in minutes."

"I will watch them from the street, Mario. I must see someone now."

"But see him in an hour."

Natale smiled and shook his head. "I must go now." He wanted to kiss Mario: the love he felt for all. He stepped through the open window into the dark heavy parlor of velvet and lace, then downstairs to the restaurant.

The doorway was suddenly illuminated by a phosphorescent flash as the night's first flare exploded in the sky. Three steps into the street and it burned out against the crowd's great OOOoooooo. He was alive again, smiling, as he walked, at the sanctimony of his own desperate prayers an hour before as he trembled at the shrine of San Gennaro. Already the entire affair—letter from Rocco, visit with Tedesco, proposal, threat—everything had begun to fade and he went now to bring simple word of Sempione's arrest to Tedesco, and to bid him goodnight.

Tedesco was alone. Delicate steam-puff snores broke from his lips like invisible smoke rings as he slept, his head snapped over the edge of his chair's backrest. One hand still grasped the demi-tasse whose contents obviously had failed to sober him and keep him awake. A bottle of anisette was half empty in his other hand. The strega was finished. The undertaker had gone.

Natale cleared his throat. He smiled as Tedesco's breathing and snoring faltered through two cycles and then returned to the normality of his sleep. The packet of money and the passport had been taken from the table. Natale considered writing a note and leaving it between Tedesco's fingers. But the wolves would not be called off Pietro till Tedesco was awake. Natale went to the door. He opened it and slammed it shut, hard.

Tedesco stirred.

"Colonel," Natale said. "Excuse me, Colonel, it is I, Natale."

The eyes opened quickly. Tedesco straightened up in the chair and belched. He drank off the cold remaining coffee in a single draft and glanced at Natale as he poured more anisette to warm his stomach.

"You are back early," he said. "The decision was not hard to reach, eh, Collector?"

Natale smiled. "No decision was reached on my part,

Colonel. Guido Sempione is in jail." In a few words he described what had happened at the Festa. "On my part it is for the good," Natale said. "I have no heart for homicide."

"On your part it is for the good." Tedesco mimicked Natale's words. "And on my part?" he demanded. "And on the part of Rocco? And the Government?" He pushed away the bottles and cup before him and got to his feet. His belt was undone and his trousers were open at the waist.

"Excuse me, Colonel," Natale said quietly, "excuse me. But now it is out of my hands. It would be difficult to reach a man behind bars. Are we in accord?"

"No, we are not in accord. What do you expect to happen now? Tell me." Tedesco fastened his clothing about him and ran his fingers through his hair.

"I have no idea. Nor do I want one. I know this thing I was called upon to do is drawn up now. I want to go home to my son. I want now to forget this episode and the margin by which I have escaped taking this animal's life, odious as it is. Our contract, so to speak, comes to nothing, touched by fate. I salute you, Colonel, and will write to Rocco in the morning. Good night."

Natale walked toward the door. Behind him there was silence. Then a drawer was pulled and a hammer smashed to the table. "Collector." Natale turned. The hammer was a gun. Its grip was by the table's edge near him, and the barrel pointed at Tedesco's chest. "Take this machine, Collector," Tedesco said evenly. "The job will be done this night, as planned. Come, come on. Kill me with it. Your eyes are plain to read. And find your dearest son in four pieces on your doorstep. Fill your pockets with this goodness, Don Natale, and sit down." He pointed to the chair before the table. Then he stepped around and went to the telephone on the sideboard by the door.

He dialed a number from memory. He tapped his foot as he waited for the receiver to be lifted on the other end, and Natale heard it when it was: "Consulato Italiano."

"The Secretary. Quickly," Tedesco ordered.

Silence. Then, "Pronto."

"He was taken by the police less than half an hour ago," Tedesco said to the telephone. His voice was like a bar of steel. He examined his wristwatch. "It is now midnight less twenty. He must be released before twelve-thirty. You know where to call." He replaced the instrument. He was calm. He returned to the other side of the table and sat down as at a desk. He smiled amiably. "Ah, Don Natale. See how the most severe complications can be cleared with a pointed call." He was like a doctor near the end of a consultation, giving heart to a patient. He took a pen from his breast pocket and a piece of paper from his wallet pad. "See how lucky you are. Now let me write for you the information you will need."


"Disturbing the peace, disorderly conduct, criminal obscenity, slander, blasphemy. Anything else you can think of, Tim?"

The two policemen laughed. The fat one said, "Resisting arrest, Sarge. It took three swings to bring 'im down."

"Goddamn radical wop! Even looks like a radical—the beard, the hat . . ."

"He lost his glasses, Sarge. Don't forget the glasses."

"Why don't you go back where you came from, you

don't like things the way they are? Go back to your friend Mussolini. At least get the hell out of New York. You goddamn radical foreigners all alike. Get in front of a crowd and you can't keep your mouth shut. Get 'em before the law and they haven't a word to say. Well, you're entitled to a telephone call. Go make it."

Sempione looked up from the gray splintered wood floor. His head hung like lead, heavy and thick on his neck, and his split lip would take seven stitches, easy. "Already all those I care about, they know where I am, Sergeant. In ten minutes every working man in this city, he knows what happened tonight. And he doesn't forget. Just so much you push. You make big mistake tonight, you cops. You think you knock me down, you put me in jail, you shut my mouth and knock out the brains of the others." Sempione smiled. "You don't have nightstick big enough to break the backs of men with nothing to lose, with strength in their will." He raised his manacled hands above his great chest and slammed the steel against the rail before him. The two policemen at his side swiftly grabbed his arms. "You do not trust the bracelets you have blessed me with this night? I do not blame you. Two, three days I spend in your stinking jail and then I talk and write again."

"All right, shut up, you guinea radical," Sergeant yelled. "No more of that Wobbly talk in this station house." He turned to the fat policeman. "Put 'im the hell away, Tim. And we'll add insulting a police officer right here." He wrote on the paper before him.

They slammed him in a single cell that looked upon the room with the bench where the Sergeant sat high above the floor behind a school-wood desk. The two cops left. Sergeant behind the desk picked up a newspaper and read with a mumbling mouth. Like a child deprived of liberty by father irate, by father embarrassed by child who tells all before invited company, Guido Sempione sat in the celled-in corner and suddenly became aware of the hand extended to him through the tight bars.

"Mr. Sempione, my name is Sean O'Neil. I'm a newspaperman too."

Sempione nodded but did not take the hand. "Go back to work," he said.

Sergeant at the desk looked up from his paper. "Try making friends with those bastards they'll chew your arm off right to the shoulder, Sean. That's the same sonofabitch that led the Commie parade in Madison Square Garden a couple of years ago."

Sean smiled. "That was more than a couple of years ago. When was it, 1916, 1917?" he asked Sempione.

"Go look it up in your newspaper file. I am not a historian."

"He's a wise-ass is what he is, Sean."

"Leave him alone, Sergeant, please, I'd like to talk to him."

"No stories tonight, Mister," Sempione said, "for a reason I do not comprehend, my head, it is hurting me."

"I'm sorry," Sean said. "Do you want a drink of water?"

"Forget it, you are not getting to me, understood? Go back to your office, go to sleep, go away. I have nothing of interest to say to you." The anger was controlled, Sempione showing no offense at the insults presented out of ignorance and fear, his beating, his jailing.

Sean O'Neil turned away. "The shit this man has been made to eat," he said to himself. He found a chair in the corner of the station house and rested his feet on top of the cold pale green radiator, and thought about Guido Sempione, his face bloody, silent in a cell behind him. "The things we've done to get him off our back."

He thought of the frontpage editorial Sempione had written in his paper in the early Twenties. "Down With Monarchy" it was called, a seven-alarm attack on Mussolini and Fascism. It wasn't the first time he had criticized Il Duce in language everybody could understand, but that particular piece had stung the Italian Government badly. Copies were smuggled into Italy and passed from hand to hand to just about everyone who could read.

Sean recalled the dinner held shortly after that paper had appeared: a formal dinner in the Waldorf Astoria, far from Sempione's beat. A lot of brass from Washington, people from the State Department, and the Italian Ambassador gave out medals to loyal Italo-Americans and made a speech about the everlasting friendship between Italy and America. But before he was through, the Ambassador complained about a certain newspaper in New York, an Italian language newspaper that was printing unflattering things about the Imperial Government, and expressed his ardent desire to see prohibitions placed in the way of the persons responsible.

His protest was forwarded by the State Department to the Postmaster General, and an Italian-speaking agent was placed in the office of *The Ax*, Sempione's newspaper, to search out some irregularity on which he could be jailed.

These things Sean had learned from friends at *The New York Dispatch* and from a senior officer in the Police Department. A month or two later, Sempione was charged with sending obscene matter through the mails: an advertisement in his paper, two lines deep, for an Italian edition of a book on birth control.

Sean lit another cigarette and shifted his feet on the radiator. Sempione was arrested and sentenced to a year in the Atlanta Penitentiary. So anxious was the government to be rid of Sempione, the prosecutor in the case, an Assistant District Attorney named Dunhill, Sean remembered, openly told the court no prison sentence would be asked if Sempione agreed to leave the country. Three days later, Sempione was locked in a cell in Atlanta, imprisoned for being a radical, for stirring up the workers all those years, for leading strikers out of factories and losing money for the bosses.

The telephone suddenly rang in the police station. Sergeant swung the receiver from its hook.

"Fifth Precinct, Sergeant Edwards. Oh good evening, sir. Yes sir, already booked. Sir? Yes sir. Right away. Good night, sir." He replaced the receiver. "Sonofabitch." He stood up at his desk and shouted "Hey Tim. Throw that bastard out on his Red ass." He turned to Sean. "Figure that one out. He goes free—no bail, no bond. Orders from the top."

Sempione moved without a word, nodding as he came within inches of Sean's face, his hyperopic vision blurred without the aid of glasses, steel rims snapped and twisted in the torn pocket of his coat; and Sean said goodnight.

When he was gone, Sean turned to Sergeant. "Shouldn't somebody give him a hand home?" he asked. "He's blind as a bat without his specs."

"Would you like to use my telephone to get him a taxi? Or do you suggest I drive him home in a prowl car?" Sergeant asked. "Do you know where that mother's on his way to now?"

Sean laughed. "Back to his office to make bombs."

Sergeant nodded. "Back to his office to make trouble," he said. "Every night before saying his prayers, he writes a column for his Commie sheet describing what he calls the injustices of the day."

"He'll have no shortage of material tonight," Sean said. He went to the door. "Maybe I'll just walk along behind him to be sure he gets where he's going all right. You wouldn't want him hit by a car. Not in your precinct anyhow."

"I'd get a medal for him stiff on my streets. Go on, get out into the cool fresh night. It's a walk you're wanting, and a glass of beer. If he spits on the sidewalk, give the sonofabitch a summons is what I'd do."

Indeed the night was cool and fresh. A breeze blew gently, brushing Sean's face like a satin curtain. He walked slowly, to keep the distance of a block between Sempione and himself a constant one, his hands behind his back, clasped. He fell into step with the one he followed, and soon he moved along like the caboose of a train rather than under his own steam. Sempione turned the corner; Sean did. Sempione crossed the street; Sean did. He could not believe the Italian did not know he was being tailed.

"Unless he doesn't care," Sean mused. "I'm not in his way at all, and he'll be rid of me when he gets to his office. 'The injustices of the day.' " He thought of how Sempione would describe the night more strongly to indict his enemies. Would he begin with the speech of Mike Volpo, king of the pin-ball machines, and the racketeers backing him for Assemblyman? Or with the unwarranted beating he took at the hands of New York police? "Probably with a rap at Volpo," Sean decided. "A clubbing by the cops isn't news in his paper anymore. He'll bring it in to show Volpo's got city protection, and not for pity for himself."

Ahead, Sempione stopped to light a cigar. He turned to avoid the breeze and cupped his hands about the match whose sudden orange phosphorescence peered through the cage of his fingers like a candle in a distant window. Instead of waiting, Sean continued toward him, wanting suddenly to end the charade. Then the match was out and Sean saw the glowing tip of the cigar for an instant and then Sempione turned his back and continued on his way and the glow disappeared. Halfway down the block Sean caught up with its autumn scent that waited suspended in the night six feet above the ground like an invitation to talk. He quickened his pace.

Just beyond a silver pool of light that flooded the street beneath a lamppost, Sempione stopped and Sean saw that glowing end of cigar move toward the curb on his left, but not to cross the street. There was a car parked there, Sean saw now, and Sempione stopped to talk to its occupant.

He slowed down as he approached the lamppost, hesitant to pass Sempione as he talked at the curb. Suddenly the old man's head was silhouetted against a blaze of razor flame as three shots exploded as rapidly as a trigger could be squeezed, and Sempione was slammed away. With an angry roar, the car lurched forward and sped by Sean as he raced to it through the lamppost's light, the glimpse of a yellow flower in that car like a brand name on the edge of his mind. A bartender with apron flopping like the frantic wings of a white bird bore down from the corner saloon and hovered bewildered as Sean searched for the heart of the man who lay in the street. Guido Sempione was dead.

# CHAPTER 5

PIETRO SIGHED. The sun was slowly melting across the Italian sky, leaving behind streaks of crimson and blue. Soon he would be with his father. "I know far too much," he said again, and Giorgio looked away as if to say he was not interested, that whatever Pietro knew beyond what he himself had learned from Natale was insignificant. "I speak of things that happened after he was gone, things you cannot know about, things purposely omitted from letters in order to spare him grief."

Giorgio nodded in approval of the consideration the innocuous letters from America had shown his brother; he had read them all.

"You speak of confession," Pietro said quietly. "For twenty years I have done penance for him without the luxury of confession. Tonight I leave purgatory at the risk of going to hell."

Giorgio smiled a little. "Tell me what was never written in those letters," he said at last. "Make your confession to me, not to your father."

"Oh Christ, what's the use," Pietro muttered in English.

83

Giorgio urged him to talk.

The day after the Festa, he had walked home from school through the still and barren streets under the erector-set arcs which the evening before had jumped in the air high over his head like the magic crown of the queen of light.

"Poor San Gennaro," he had mused. If Pappa were San Gennaro, he would keep the Festa alive forever. The streets would never be dark, people would dance there and sing, the wheels would spin every night, red balloons would fill the sky. To cry would be against the law. If Zia Emilia were San Gennaro, everybody would embroider pillowcases and be paid twenty-five cents each.

Maybe Pappa would be a saint someday. Santo Natale. People said it already: holy Christmas. He remembered the saying Pappa had taught him a few nights before. "Mi chiamo Sbagliato, ma non mi sbaglio." Pietro said it aloud there in broad daylight in Italian, in front of the undertaker's clock. Twelve-fifteen. He began to walk faster. "Sbagliato means mistaken in English," Pappa had said, "but we are not mistaken. Remember that always."

And yet Pappa had not kissed him in his bed last night. Or maybe he had been asleep when he'd come to touch his face lightly, his breath rich with the scent of smoke and red wine, his chin scratchy like the sleeves of a sweater. He was already out in the morning before Pietro's breakfast of warm milk and bread prepared by Zia Emilia muttering to herself. With sudden joy, Pietro remembered other times Pappa had been gone in the morning; those times had brought him home for lunch the following day.

He began to run.

Nick the druggist's son raced past him. On the other sidewalk, Luigi the barber, no coat over his white jacket and pants, ran toward Grand Street and turned the corner there. Pietro laughed to see Luigi run, he was like a girl throwing a ball.

In a minute, people rushed from doorways shouting and ran like Nick and Luigi. Was there a fire? Had someone been hit by a car? Pietro ran faster around the corner.

Two police cars, like green and white arrows, stuck out from the curb halfway down the block, and it was to them everyone ran as though to pull them away and throw them back where they came from.

He was not sure which building the police had gone into, having left one of themselves to guard the cars against the crowd, to sit without expression as dark eyes and ragged hair peered through the windows at the unintelligible bits of words that sputtered from the short-wave radio, alive for a glimpse of riot guns or tear-gas bombs, to listen to the babbled questions. "What happened?" "Somebody commit suicide?" "Can you make the siren go when you're not moving?" To Pietro, it was like another festa, with excitement and laughter and owners away from the shops.

"They're in *your* house," a boy's voice called, and diverted Pietro's attention from the spinning red light atop the car to the entrance of his building. There was another policeman there, tall before the peeling brown door, his hands on his hips, nightstick dangling from leather thong wrapped around his wrist, "G'wan home, it's none of your business, g'wan back to work," this one said over and over again to the silent ones his redfaced hulk towered over.

They opened a path before Pietro as he forced his way through them, knowing him as the son of Don Natale who lived in that building. And still the policeman would not let him pass, till an old man grabbed away the books from Pietro's hands and thrust them labeled with name and address close to the hard blue eyes and made him turn and check the fading numbers on the cracked glass behind him.

Pietro opened the door and screams from the floors above tumbled down on him, and he fell on the first few steps of the stairs and scraped his knees.

"Pappa. Pappa," he called out and he knew he was crying. "Pappa."

"Stinking cops, putrefying guts of pig."

"Leave us. Go before we throw you from the roof."

"Sausage stuffed with dung. We'll rip you apart and sow you in the streets."

"Pappa. Zia Emilia," Pietro screamed, and his voice was dream-like in his ears, barely audible though his throat burned with his screams as he clambered up the stairs.

Every door in the hall was opened and framed, like abject Stations of the Cross, the agony of Italians stranded there in fury as they shrieked their tongue of imprecation at the lone policeman on the floor above, standing frightened guard before Don Natale's door.

"Pietro, Pietro, bring heart to her tortured soul."

"Dear one, comfort her, that woman of Christ."

And they reached out and touched him as he ran by, relic of a future saint.

From the quiet rooms of his house crashed Zia Emilia's sudden scream. They were killing her, she threatened to jump from a window if they did not leave her alone. She was dressed in black seated on a kitchen chair, pushed away from the embroidery frame. Her face was wet and red with tears and anger, and Pietro ran to her and her arms wrapped him to her and together they cried.

"This must be his kid."

"Must be."

"Why don't you take a look in the bedroom and see if you can find anything?"

Pietro pushed himself away from his aunt in time to see a policeman enter Pappa's room. "What, what is it they want?" he whispered, and Zia Emilia wiped away his tears with the black-edged handkerchief balled in her hand. A big man dressed in gray, an American, leaned against the sink and smoked a cigarette and stared at the floor.

"Do not be afraid, Pietro mio," Zia Emilia said with trembling voice, and she kissed his forehead. "They ask for your father Natale. What man with work is home this time of day? I cannot make them understand."

The big man turned water on in the sink and wet his cigarette and dropped it into the bag of garbage in the pail by the stove. He touched Pietro's shoulder gently and nodded at the schoolbooks on the table. "You go to school," he said. He smiled. "You speak English?"

"Yes."

"Please tell your mother I am not a policeman. I work for a newspaper."

"She is my aunt." Pietro told Zia Emilia what the big man said.

She nodded her head hard. "Animale," she muttered. "Ask him what they want with your father. Has something happened?"

"Nothing happened to him," the big man said quietly to Pietro's question. "The police just want to talk to him. Have you seen your father today?"

"No."

"What does he say?" Zia Emilia asked.

Pietro told her.

"When was the last time you saw him?"

"Last night. At the Festa."

"What time?"

Pietro shrugged his shoulders and asked Zia Emilia.

"Who knows?" she said angrily. "Nine, nine-thirty?"

The policeman came from Natale's room carrying four or five notebooks and a small leather case. "I'll handle the questions if you don't mind, Sean. You've got no business being here as it is."

"Without my lead you wouldn't be here in the first place. Let me see what you've got there."

The shouting in the hall had died.

The big man called Sean leafed through the books the policeman had found. "Numbers." The policeman opened the black case. It was lined with red velvet and held, like a jewel, a small silver pistol with a mother-of-pearl handle. He checked its empty magazine and examined the hammer. "Never been fired."

"Tell the bastards your father kills flies with it," Zia Emilia said.

Pietro told them.

"Smart-ass wop," the policeman said.

"Where is my father?"

The policeman set the silver gun back in its case and walked to the window. "Does your father ever wear a flower in his buttonhole?" he asked.

Pietro nodded. "So do I."

"Sean, look at this," the policeman said from the window. He had discovered the box of chrysanthemums and basil on the fire escape.

"There they are," Sean said. "Grows his own." He raised the window for a better look.

"Now it is against the law to grow flowers in this country," Zia Emilia mumbled.

"What she say?" the policeman asked. "Tell her she could get a summons for having that box out there. Wouldn't be funny if it fell and crowned somebody passing by."

Sean picked a yellow chrysanthemum and lowered his head to sniff the basil. As he did, his eyes raced along the facade of buildings along the south side of the street. Flower boxes jutted out from the tenement face like buckteeth of gold. "Oh sweet Jesus," he said.

"What's wrong?" the policeman asked and looked out the window. "I better check out those flats," he said.

"Bring cops into all those buildings and there'd be a revolution down here," Sean said shaking his head. "Forget it." He put on his hat and turned to Pietro. "Tell your aunt we're sorry to bother you." He patted Pietro's shoulder. "Be a good boy in school," he said, and to Emilia he tipped his hat and said goodbye. The policeman followed him to the door, books and gun case under his arm.

"That you break your legs on the stairs," Zia Emilia called after them.

"Same to you, lady," the policeman said.

As soon as the two were in the hall, swearing from the open doors began again and serenaded them down to the street.

Zia Emilia crushed her hands together in a double fist at her clenched eyes, lips tight, and whispered "Eternal Father" deep in her breath, "I take this vow: if I do not give him a pulling of ears he will never forget, tonight I take poison." She slammed her hands with such force against the embroidery frame, the one-by-two she struck splintered like a toothpick and all five pieces crashed to the floor, held together by the pillowcase she had been working on.

"Wait," she screamed, "wait, just wait for that pig to return to this house. Leaving us to be taken for brigands in the kitchen I keep him." She aimed her heavy head at Pietro. "Why, why the tears anew? Because you are frightened or because you see father of yours away from home stinking of goat?"

"Sainted Emilia," cried Cumare Maria from the doorway. "Why do you take it with this heart of God? What fault is it of his Natale is not here, that policemen curse this house with blue-coated presence? This son of mother can still be held in arms," she said, embracing Pietro, kissing his hot cheeks. "Leave him alone. See how he has hurt his knee."

Zia Emilia kneeled before the boy and kissed him. "When did you do this thing to yourself?" she asked gently. "Enough, enough tears. Answer your aunt."

"Finish it, do me this favor," Cumare Maria said. She wet a dish towel with steaming hot water and carried it to Pietro's bruised knee. "A blind man could see that he fell. Is it not enough?" With one hand she washed the scraped skin and with the other she caressed his face.

By the time the towel was cool, he had stopped crying. "I will be late for school," he said, sensing somehow he would not be made to go back for the afternoon.

Zia Emilia wiped his face with the clean side of the towel. "Remain at home for my company the rest of this day. Your father has made a beautiful lesson no teacher could . . ."

"Emilia." Cumare Maria tapped her foot. "Leave it alone."

Maria had left the front door open and through it now, as through the open gate of a canal, steamed the armada that had gathered on stairs and halls, waiting for her absence to signal they could pass.

Fat Anna came first, a powerful tugboat. Then Serafina the Gaunt, white like the mercy of a hospital ship, carrying a medicine bottle with a finger of cognac for Emilia's reinforcement. Big-breasted Teresa was next, the cruiser. Pepina, called to her face The Nun, drifted in the wake of Lisabetta. Donna Matilda, who once could recite a poem in Latin, was last.

They churned through the kitchen.

"What did the vermin seek, in the house of Don Natale?"

"Pray to the Virgin they do not return."

"The bastards, they come to break the horns of an honest Christian and the soul of God."

"Thanks to Paradise they left you whole."

"I would put them head to head to be cracked like nuts."

"Take this drop of cognac, that it gives you force."

Zia Emilia embraced them one by one. "Without coffee, not even cognac would get past my throat, so dry is it from nerves." She took down the macchinetta of twelve cups and set water on the stove to boil. "Ah, Santo

Natale." She bit her hand. "It is not the first night he passes away from his home and son. But this time he will pay for it."

Teresa laughed loud and held her hands to her breast. "He paid for it last night for all you know."

"Show us the three centimes, cow," said Fat Anna, and Teresa let go her breast and pointed at Fat Anna and laughed and laughed.

"ZZZZzzzzzz, if you please," whispered The Nun. "In front of the child?"

Zia Emilia took cups from the cupboard. "Stinking of wine, some fallen pig on his arm, and he the cavaliere cock."

"Emilia, Emilia," Serafina sighed, nodding her head, "go not too hard with him. Young is he still, six years without wife . . ."

The Nun made the Sign of the Cross. "That the Eternal Father keep her."

". . . saint he never was."

"But must he bring police to call each time he relieves himself?" Emilia went to the window. In the now empty street, on the other sidewalk, she saw the big man Sean. "Still is he there, that one, cigarette in mouth, waiting to peddle his papers."

Teresa ran to her side. She threw open the window. She brushed black hair from her eyes. "Hey you police-a-man," she cried in English, and then in Italian, "up your ass, you and your mother." She gave him the sign.

"Ecco Mario," Donna Matilda said, announcing the cafe-keeper's arrival. "Tell us, where have you hidden Don Natale?"

Mario addressed himself to Emilia. "I came as quickly as I could. Look, I did not even take away my apron. What happens here?"

Zia Emilia told him of the police and their inquiries after her brother, whom she cursed. "Now do not remove your apron, Mario," she said, "you are in time to bring professional hand to my kitchen. Make the coffee, if you please, eh?"

"Have you not brought along a dozen pastries to sweeten this bitter afternoon?" Fat Anna asked.

"Quickly, give us a taste of your connollo," cried Teresa.

"But what is it with Big Tits here today?" asked Cumare Maria.

"Run to where your man spills his blood at work," Lisabetta said as she wiped tears of laughter from her eyes, "and give him a special sandwich for his lunch."

"Jesus, Mary, and Joseph." The Nun closed her eyes in Pietro's direction, expecting a miracle to remove him from the vulgarity of that room.

A knock at the door silenced them. Zia Emilia straightened up from the cups she set on the table and Pietro took hold of her skirt. "Who comes now in the name of God?"

Mario took off his apron and opened the door.

In the hall, an old woman waited with a covered dish in her hands. She stepped forward and looked swiftly about the kitchen and found Zia Emilia. She nodded her kerchiefed white head, offering the dish across the room.

"Ah, Missus Kapilana," Zia Emilia said in English, "come in, come in," urging with her hands the back-rooms neighbor to enter.

Mrs. Kaplan shook her head and smiled. "I must go to my son in the store." She handed over the dish. "I saw the police." She paused, her next words uncertain. "You have no trouble I wish."

"Little bit, nothing big."

"This morning I make cake. The boy likes cake?" and she smiled at Pietro.

Zia Emilia thanked the old woman. Their gazes caught and they were together in a sudden embrace.

"Stay for coffee," Teresa called. "Stay for coffee, one minute it takes."

But Mrs. Kaplan could not stay, explaining her son waited at the store for his lunch, and she backed out the door, smiling and nodding like an Italian in her want of English.

Zia Emilia seized from the table the ring of dried figs purchased the evening before at the Festa. "Missus Kapilana!" She ran to the stairs and put the loop of tough straw in the old woman's hand.

A smile, a nod, acceptance.

The kitchen was silent when she returned, and Mario filled the macchinetta with boiling water. Zia Emilia sat down and lifted Pietro to her lap. "What is more, she lost her husband last year," she said softly, rocking the boy, "poor Christian."

With short swift sips they drank the strong steaming coffee. Before they were through, Luigi the barber arrived. He was long in coming, he explained, because he had stayed in the street to get the full story, knowing Emilia would be surrounded and cared for by the very group of esteemed ladies he saw before him now. He made a little bow to Mario. "You forgive me of course, Mario, I do not count you with my words."

"If you had come five minutes earlier," Lisabetta said, "you would have seen him tied in apron strings like a pregnant one seven months to the good."

Big-breasted Teresa stood next to the barber. She sniffed his pomaded hair. "And you, sweet one, scented like a dance hall, would have been the midwife, prepared as you are with tools of your profession." In a single motion, she stole scissors and comb from his pocket and snipped air before Mario's belly, tied the imaginary cord, and pushed its knot with her thumb hard below his waist.

Only The Nun did not laugh, and with resignation she folded her hands in her lap. She cleared her throat. "Emilia," she said quietly, "on my part, I am not offended. But the poor soul of God you hold to your heart has already heard enough to burn the ears of the devil himself."

Teresa threw up her hands. "Oo fa. And what have I said to offend you?"

The Nun lowered her eyes. "I do not take it with you, Teresina," she said quietly.

Zia Emilia shook her head at Teresa to signal acquiescence. "All right, all right, you are right." She put Pietro's feet to the floor and kissed him. "Go, son of aunt, study your lessons this day free from school."

"When does Pappa come?"

"Soon, my heart, soon. Here, take the cake the good Jew brought you."

Pietro gone from the room, Mario grabbed Teresa round her waist and slapped with open hand her tight hard ass. "That for your abortive delivery," he cried. He kissed his hand and pressed it to his chest. "But I would let myself be taken by you still again for another taste of that delicious tail."

"He even talks screwing like a cook," Teresa screamed, and their laughter rang into the parlor where Pietro settled by the window at which, just the night before, he had sat in Pappa's lap and listened to the story of the other side.

He took the waxed paper from the old woman's dish. It was a small piece of cake, and he had eaten no lunch. He rose from the chair, to ask Zia Emilia if it was meant all for him. Instead he broke it in two. It was warm. It smelled not of soup, like the old woman who smiled at him with never a word and who had brought him this good sweet cake, but of raisins and nuts and fruit. He wrapped the second piece in the crinkled paper and took it to Pappa's room where Pappa would see it when he came home, even if he came after he, Pietro, was in bed.

He stopped at the open door of the bedroom. Every drawer was open wide, as they never were when Pappa was there. Shirts, underwear, socks, pajamas, everything had been pulled from Pappa's place and left thrown where it had fallen. The policeman had done this while the big one had kept them with his questions in the kitchen. He was afraid to go in, for Pappa must see this mess the policeman had made. The policeman would be punished. And yet Pappa would return tired and anxious for his bed.

He set the cake down on the bureau, next to the picture of the mother he had never known, and returned the clothing to its place. Shirts in one drawer, underwear and socks in another. How big the clothes were. They felt of his father. In one of the drawers the policeman had found the gun. "Tell the bastards your father kills flies with it," Zia Emilia had said. Pappa had never let him have a cap pistol to play with, but he had a real gun of his own. Pappa lit matches for cigars, too.

By the parlor window he ate the cake. It was gone with three bites. He thought of the dried figs from the Festa. They were gone now, too. He went back to Pappa's room and broke in half the cake he had left on the bureau. There was still a taste for Pappa who never ate before going to bed. And Pappa would return after bedtime, he was certain of that now. One time, they had been without Pappa for two days. Zia Emilia had not talked to Pappa a long time after that. But then he had made her laugh and they were friends again. And now Pappa was gone again and the police had come looking for him. The last time, Zia Emilia had gone looking for him too. This time the policemen were helping her look and she had screamed at them, and everybody had come.

Children ran in the street. School was out for the day. He had missed the afternoon and had got nothing out of staying home.

"Arrivederci," said Cumare Maria in the kitchen. "Arrivederci," said Serafina, "stay well." Pietro opened his reader. Billy runs to the store. A blond boy running on a sidewalk along the edge of red and yellow stores. Where is this American street, boys called Billy? The door closed in the hall. The stores have awnings like the carousel on the truck.

"Aaaaaa chooooo." Signor Luigi.

"Salute."

"Aaaaaaa choooo. Ahhh."

"That you keep well a hundred years."

"Is there still another drop of coffee in that beautiful pot?"

"There are even two drops."

"I thank you." Pause. "Ehhh, we think there are disturbances in this house," Signor Mario said so softly he could barely be heard in the parlor. "Consider the house of Guido Sempione this day."

"You think he is missed by that blooded Irish whore?" The barber spoke. "He leaves a wife and family on the other side unseen ten years."

"A man is entitled to pass his personal life as it

pleases him, when his public life is in the service of his brothers."

"No no no," said The Nun. "Excuse me, Mario, but in the eyes of God, we have one life and it must be lived between His lines of morality."

"However it is, Sempione burns in Hell this instant," Luigi said.

"I do not believe it."

"Then it is true," said Zia Emilia. "I had heard half a thing about his death."

"Last night. Three fusillades in the head."

"Mario, look," said The Nun patiently. "It takes but a single mortal sin . . ."

"Ooo fa," said Teresa. "They speak of good and evil and you speak of eating meat on Friday."

"Beautiful words for a Catholic."

"Say a Mass for me. Better that I take myself away before I bite my tongue. We see each other soon."

Teresa came to the parlor and kissed Pietro's face. She smelled of flowers. "Stay well, dear one," and then she too was gone. Pietro liked her best of all. She was a true aunt.

"Since we have set ourselves upon it, tell me, please," Luigi asked, "how Sempione's life was in the service of his brothers? By heaping dung on the one great leader we have had these hundred years?"

"You speak of the other side, Luigi, and I speak of us here in America."

"O, you have made yourself American now. Whiskey e soda. Bravo."

"And where are we now, in Naples? I speak of his attempt to bring dignity to those who throw their blood in labor to fill with riches the manicured hands of bankers."

"And I speak of Mussolini's attempt at bringing dignity to an entire nation, nation of your birth."

"That is the difference between Fascism and Humanitarianism."

"—and Communism, you want to say."

"I ignore you there. Look, Luigi, there are things Mussolini has done the value of which I do not question. The fact remains he is a dictator. See how he has reached across the sea and killed Sempione."

The barber laughed. "Further proof of his ability to get things done."

"Yes, trains run according to schedule, fountains flow in village squares, dialects are no longer spoken in the North."

"And the hospitals and the schools, full employment and stomachs equally full, the unity, the dignity—your word—of the New Italy? Answer me that. And Abyssinia?"

Mario did not answer for a moment. Then, "Yes, Abyssinia."

"Ahh, Mario mio, you are incurably sentimental. One is either for or against Il Duce. I shed no tears for Guido Sempione. But that it did not come to him ten years before."

"He is a greater loss to us now than Mussolini will ever be. I hope I am wrong."

"Take yourself to bed," Luigi said, "you do not reason."

"Look," said Zia Emilia, "it is better that you end this song. Discussions of politics, as with religion, never arrive at the finish."

"Si si si." The Nun's mouse voice. "You speak truth. Why? Because with religion, it is . . ."

"She counted religion," Lisabetta interrupted.

99

"Come little sister mine. I will take you to your house."

They left, and minutes later Luigi pushed his chair away from the table. "That Nun turns every sidewalk into the road to Calvary. Emilia, I have sorrow for your disturbance this day. In five minutes, the collector returns with a symphony of hammers playing between his ears, listen to me. Mario, think a little of what we talked. Arrivederci. Donna Matilda, arrivederci."

In a while the old woman left too, and only Mario stayed on with Zia Emilia in the kitchen. He smoked a cigar now, Pietro knew, for its smoke drifted into the parlor. The room smelled like when Pappa was home.

"Go home, Mario," Zia Emilia said gently. "It is not necessary that you stay."

"This is a quiet hour at the restaurant," Mario said. "I keep you company until Natale comes. You have not one idea where he could be?"

"It is not that he is not here that fills my head," Emilia said. "The Virgin knows he has passed more than one night in a bed not his own. But the sainted visit of the police, Mario."

Mario laughed. "Remember, in this country it is prohibited to collect miserable centimes for the lottery. Who knows? It is possible Natale forgot his weekly payment to the law, and all at once they become scrupulous. This matter will be settled with a bill of ten dollars, listen to me."

Zia Emilia sighed. "Have you desire for more coffee?"

"I thank you, no."

Across the street, Artie came out of the grocery store with a loaf of Sicilian bread and a bottle of milk.

Pietro considered the remaining piece of cake in Pappa's room.

From the kitchen came the click of the radio on top of the icebox. "Let us listen to a little music," Mario said. "Perhaps we catch ourselves a ballad of Carlo Butti."

> *. . . colla bionda e colla nera,*
> *Me ne vado a passegiar'.*
> *E beh, e beh,*
> *L'ai voluto te.*
> *E beh, e. . . .*

The music—the singing, the guitar—was suddenly cut.

"Damnit," Zia Emilia said angrily. "It did the same thing yesterday."

> *Signore e signori . . .*

"See, it takes only a curse to return it to life."

> *. . . l'ultimo bollettino attineto a*
> *l'assassinamento di Guido Sempione.*

"Poor Christian," Zia Emilia murmured.

> *. . . rivelato il primo sospetto d'essere*
> *uno Natale Sbagliato, Uno, Sei, Due, Zero Grand*
> *Street . . .*

"AAAAAAAAIII DIO NO!"
"EMILIA!"

"ZIA ZIA!"

Chair knocked over, she lay stiff on white tile floor of kitchen, eyes like quarters, mouth open wide, hands fisted at her head.

"Quickly. Get Doctor Fonso," Mario shouted.

When he reached the doctor's office, Pietro was unable to speak.

# CHAPTER 6

GIORGIO STOOD UP and seemed to shiver. The day was still warm though the sun had begun to dip beyond the hills across the way. "She used to be the quiet one," he said, shaking his head in disbelief at Pietro's account of Emilia's hysteria. "She was the saint of the family, the little sister of charity. She used to pass entire days in the country, in stinking huts with grass-thatched roofs, caring for peasants too sick and old to care for themselves. Never once did I hear her raise her voice, neither in anger nor joy."

"Then it is difficult for you to imagine what she was like those first days," Pietro said. "She would be working in the kitchen, cooking or doing her embroidery, and she would look at me and suddenly begin to cry, so softly at first you could barely hear her. Her eyes would fill with tears, and then the tears would stream down her face and then she sobbed aloud, great sobs that seemed to explode in her heart. And then she would moan, and the moaning moved quickly into a loud call to God or the saints, there was never any difference between them for her, and then she would be screaming and pulling at her hair as no answer came from above.

"I used to stay out of her way as much as possible. It is not a good feeling to have the unwitting ability to push someone to the very edge of reason every time you come within sight. I felt like the ghost of my father.

"Anyway, they kept me at Mario's house for a while until Zia Emilia recovered from the shock, until she stopped screaming and pulling at her hair. The night they brought me back to the house, they undressed me in Pappa's room and put me to bed between his sheets. I was frightened, because to sleep in his bed meant he was not expected home that night either."

The pillow was redolent still with the scent of Pappa's cigar. Pietro slid easily into the mold in the side of the mattress close to the windows. The other side was flat and hard like new. He stretched his feet but could not reach the edge of the deep form; it went beyond him, like the sleeves of a shirt too big. Zia Emilia and Mario were talking in the kitchen. He could hear the silver touch of their spoons against the espresso cups.

"Does he sleep?" Mario was asking quietly, and Zia Emilia answering, "Not yet, not yet." Mario drew deeply on his cigar and exhaled in a sigh. "Look, Emilia, now you must do me this favor," he said. "We must talk with our heads."

"You say the first word," Emilia answered.

"Very well." Pause. "Do you remember my sister who lives in Brooklyn, the one called Lenora? The widow?"

"Eh beh—so what?"

"She asks always of you."

"See if he gets where he is going," Emilia muttered.

"As you know, she has a grandson the age of Pietro. The other night I called her to know how the boy carries himself, having been sick with . . ."

"You called her? How do you call her?"

"By telephone," Mario said, "she has a telephone in the parlor. What was I saying? Ah, yes, I called her and she asked news of you, having heard the broadcasts. . . . To make it short," Mario said, "she has much sympathy and concern."

"Thank her. But what have we to do with one another's lives?" Emilia drained the last sweet drop of coffee from her cup.

"Consider it for a minute," Mario said. "She, without husband, grandson of Pietro's years, alone with six rooms in Brooklyn, yearning for companionship."

"That she marry again. What are you saying?"

"What she suggested—that you and the soul of God asleep in his father's bed go from here for the good of the boy and start anew in Brooklyn."

"Do not make me laugh."

"And do not make me lose patience. You cannot remain here. How are you to live? Who is to pay the rent and put food on your table, bring you company those long gray days of winter that terrify you so?"

Emilia rinsed the coffee cups in the sink. "It is my consideration," she said.

"No, I have already considered it," Mario said. "This is the best way."

She turned from the sink, tired eyes opened wide with anger, her mouth tight. "And what do you think I have become that I would shower a widow with tragedy that is no concern of hers?" she demanded. "What senseless pig do you take me for to dream I could burden her table with the flesh and blood of an assassin? Have you lost your senses? Get out of here before I put two cold hands about your throat."

"Without dramatics, please," Mario said. "This was to be a sensible discussion, not an opera."

"Then do not talk like an imbecile."

Mario remained silent as Emilia took up her embroidery frame and set it between the kitchen table and the window sill. She had bound the broken stake with a splint fashioned from a mushroom basket, and twine. Mario examined the joint as she pinned in the edge of a yellow linen tablecloth. "Tomorrow I will bring you a new arm," he said quietly, "this one will not hold for long."

Emilia nodded and pulled her chair forward and set to work.

Mario closed his eyes and puffed his cigar. He listened to Emilia's needle singing through the cloth, the phrases running shorter and shorter as the thread was consumed in the yellow breast of a bird. "Let me tell it another way," he said at last. "Please do not answer until I have said all that must be said."

"Mario, go home, do me this favor."

"Damnit," he shouted angrily. Then he remembered Pietro in the other room and lowered his voice. "You cannot remain here," he said again, "even if there was not the question of money, you could not remain here." He paused for an instant and then cruelly went on. "What will you say to the boy when he comes to you on his knees for explanation to give vindictive pups that swing round him like devils on a chain, chanting through their teeth words heard at home? The first lesson he learns on his return to school is that his father . . ."

106

"What do you know of it?" Emilia interrupted without raising her eyes from the cloth.

"Emilia," Mario said gently, "it is known, it is known. No matter what you could tell the boy at night to hide him from the truth, in the morning it would be destroyed like the tender shoot by early frost. In Brooklyn you would not be known. Pietro would be another boy in his class.

"Think of how he loves that father. Think of which is best for the boy—that his mind be pounded by the hammer of truth, or that he be permitted to mature as others, believing with the blind faith of a child his father is more man than he is. My own children, Emilia, see me as a kind of Christ, granting privileges, controlling their entire world. They must believe this, just as we must believe in God. Do not allow the God of that boy to be taken from him, Emilia, for the sin of it falls on your head."

She had set her needle still, like a guidon with threaded pennant flowing, at the edge of white plumage in the bird she invented with her loop stitch. Her eyes were shut, her face immobile. Now tears flowed slowly down her cheeks as from the varnished lids of an icon touched by a miracle.

"And why do you cry?" Mario asked gently. "Do you not see this is the best way?"

Emilia shook her head. "You do not know the boy. The lie will never satisfy him."

"Ah, Emilia. You do not understand the mind of children. When they ask where the stars spend the day, there is no need to be an astronomer to explain. When they ask if the soul of a kitten killed by a car goes to heaven, your answer is better than that of a priest. They

107

know not truth; they seek only reassurance. Reassure this God's child. Keep from him the knowledge that a mother gives birth in pain, that hunger kills, that the best of men make the irrevocable mistakes they were born to make. Do not destroy the fantasy of a child's world. Soon enough will he learn the truths that burden us all to the grave."

Emilia did not answer right away, and when she did, she said simply, "I will not delude him as his father did. I will not run away in shame."

That was the end of it. Mario left, Zia Emilia went to bed, and Pietro, having understood little more than Mario had wanted them to go to live in a place called Brooklyn, fell asleep wondering what it was Zia Emilia would not run away from.

That night, in his sleep, he saw a long hallway with a door at its end. From behind that door, Pappa called to him in a closeted voice. Desperately he tried to reach that door but could not lift his feet. Then in his dream he screamed to Pappa, "Come and get me, come and get me," never hearing his own voice till he awakened in Zia Emilia's arms, she whispering gently, "Here, here I am, Pietro, here I am."

Three days later, he returned to school and the day went badly. In his absence, they had learned many new words, read many new stories in the Weekly Reader. In the afternoon, when it was his turn to stand in place and read aloud from the workbook, Miss Larson excused him and said he would have to catch up with work he had missed. He tried to follow from the big type before him the monotone voices that droned endlessly up and down the aisles, remembering Pappa's admonition that he learn his lessons well. But it was all over his head and finally

108

he gave it up and allowed his mind to slip to just this side of consciousness, vaguely aware now and then of Miss Larson's glance that seemed to him to say, "You are in trouble." When the three o'clock bell finally rang, it signaled, rather than release, preparation of homework certain to be done all wrong.

The new words and Miss Larson's look worried him as he walked home. There was nobody to help him. Zia Emilia could not even speak English, let alone read it. And who knew when Pappa would be back? Pappa did not read either, but would know how to get somebody to help. But if Pappa were home, school would not have been missed and he would not be behind in the reading.

He heard running footsteps in back of him. He turned around to see three members of the Shamrocks coming at him fast. His immediate impulse was to run. The Shamrocks were an older gang of boys, nine and ten, who took girls into the empty lot behind the gasoline station. Pietro had heard they cut off a girl's finger because she would not give up a diamond ring. But he kept walking. He hadn't done anything to them. He recognized Jimmy Costello. He used to think Jimmy was Italian because his name ended in a vowel. Jimmy's older brother was arrested once for stealing a car.

Jimmy and the other two caught up with him and they stopped running. They walked around him, Jimmy behind, the other two walking backwards in front of him. They didn't touch him, they were smiling, but Pietro was scared even though he had never done anything to them.

"What's your name, kid?" the one on the right in front asked.

"Pietro."

"What kinda name's that?" Jimmy Costello behind

109

him asked. Pietro turned around to answer him and as he did, one in front knocked his book out of his hand.

"It's a wop name," that one said, and the other one in front laughed.

"Hey, cut it out, you guys," Jimmy Costello ordered. "Whatsa big idea, knocking the kid's book outa his hands?" Jimmy bent down to help Pietro pick up the book and Pietro bent down too. Something swelling up in his throat made him afraid he was going to cry.

The sidewalk suddenly crashed up at him like a black wall in the dark.

"Now why'd ya wanna kick him for?" Jimmy asked, far away.

He could tell he was crying now, he could feel the tears streaming down his face but he made no sound. He was afraid to touch his nose, which hurt very much, because he was sure it was bleeding. The palms of his hands were scratched.

"Hey, no kiddin'," Jimmy Costello said kindly. He helped Pietro up from the sidewalk. "What kinda name's that?" He really seemed to want to know.

"Italian."

"No foolin'?"

Pietro nodded. It was all over. They would leave him alone now.

"Your father 'Talian too?" Jimmy Costello asked.

Pietro said yes. The wind was flapping the pages of his Weekly Reader. He backed around to be sure there was no one behind him.

"Where's your father now?" Jimmy Costello asked.

Pietro stooped again to recover his book.

A sneakered foot kicked it away and tore the cover off. "What're you, deaf? He asked you where's your father?"

"I don't know," Pietro cried out. The tears streamed fast now and he didn't care; there was no reason not to cry.

"Y' hear that? The little wop doesn't know where his wop father is."

"Cops don't even know where he is," Jimmy Costello said. "Tell us where your father is."

"I don't know," Pietro sobbed. Somebody shoved him from behind and he stumbled into Jimmy Costello.

"Wanna get tough, huh, y' wop bastard," Jimmy said, and with clenched fists pushed Pietro backwards against the other one who said, "I don't want 'im," and socked him forward again. Jimmy Costello held him with one hand then and with the other slapped his face. His cheek caught fire and his eyes blurred with tears. He could not see. "Pappa, Pappa," he called out to himself.

"Maybe if we aired out his brains a little bit he'll remember where his father is," one of them said and they laughed joyously and swiftly agreed to pull off his pants.

They twisted his arms behind his back and pushed him into an alley way and Jimmy Costello ripped the buttons off his fly. Pietro's lip was cut and already puffed and he could taste blood in his mouth, and the salt of his own tears and perspiration burned through the scuffed skin on his face. Suddenly he remembered the story of the girl whose finger the Shamrocks had cut off, and his fear exploded into a violent hatred and he kicked out, felt the dull thud of his shoe against the bone of Jimmy Costello's leg, heard him scream with pain. Then he kicked backward with both feet and they let go. He lunged at Jimmy Costello, caught him off guard, knocked him down and fell on top of him, his hands closed in fists for the first time in his life, punching with pleasure at the freck-

111

led face until the others rolled him onto the sidewalk and swiftly, kneeling on either side of him, beat him until he stopped moving and they were afraid they had killed him. And then they ran away.

When he opened his eyes, Pietro felt the pain of a hammer across his brow. Even without a mirror, he could see the swelling of his cheeks and nose. He had to breathe through his mouth, his lips cracked and bleeding, and he could not draw a full breath. He tried to think of the breath coming in his mouth, going down his throat, tried to push it all down into his lungs. And then he realized he was trying to keep from throwing up. He couldn't stop it. He tried to turn his face to the side but his neck hurt too much and he vomited and it rushed back down his throat and he choked and coughed and he was drowning and he knew he was going to die. "Please God, don't let me die," he heard himself croak. God would not understand what he was trying to say. He tried to call out but could only make the croaking noise.

Running feet. Jimmy Costello had come after him again. He would never tell where Pappa was. He would say he did not know. Pa. Pappa. "I don't know where he is, I don't know."

"Just take it easy, kid," somebody was saying, "we'll find out, we'll get you home. Just take it easy."

Was it worth it to fight open his eyes again? Somebody was helping him up. Ahh, how it hurt below the stomach. He touched himself there. He had wet his underwear. Could they see what he had done? There was a brick wall in front of his face. He had to go to the bathroom but could not. He had already gone, like wetting the bed. Had he wet Pappa's bed? O God, o God.

"Can you stand up?"

112

Yes, he could stand up, he was standing up. His legs buckled and big hands caught him and lifted him up, cradled him like a baby. Now he could only see the blue sky. And the blue coat of the one who held him. Police? Smart-ass wop. Where's your father? Pappa, I don't know. "I don't know where he is. Leave me alone." The sound came out of his throat.

"Just take it easy, kid, you'll be all right."

"I know where he lives. His name's Peter Sbagliato."

"This his kid? Jesus, but they beat him up good."

They were carrying him away. "I didn't do anything. Honest. I don't know where he is."

"Lay still. I'm gonna take you home."

He let his eyes close. He stopped fighting. He did not care that Zia Emilia would scream when the policeman carried him into the kitchen.

At noon the following Saturday, the truck that delivered ice to Cafe Mario waited in the street outside the house of Natale Sbagliato. Its driver, Pasquale Siciliano, remembering still Natale's payment three years before on a number played and won with an I.O.U., had dried and swept out the wagon floor and draped clean canvas inside the stake walls to keep the collector's furniture safe from marks. In a little while, Mario arrived and together they waited for Luigi. When the barber showed, they climbed the stairs slowly to the rooms to be emptied.

They carried down the icebox first, with lowered eyes and without a word, like pallbearers mindful of the pain their presence brought to Teresa and Cumare Maria and Serafina who hovered at respectful distance about Emilia and the battered boy. They emptied the collector's bedroom next, of its mahogany dressers and vanity table, the proud matrimonial bed that had served only through the birth of his son. As the men worked, the women went from room to room, filling cardboard cartons with clothes and dishes, figurines of china and ashtrays of glass, pots and pans, threadworn towels, radio and clock, half-filled packages of spaghetti, a box of salt, cans of tomatoes and bags of dried beans, a tin of olive oil.

Emilia took Mario's arm and led him into Natale's room and opened the closet there. "Look, these things I leave to your discretion," she said, and touched the sleeves of the collector's suits. "You know the fanatic he was when it came to clothes. You and he are of the same measure. Do me this last favor. I hope I do not offend you. Let me leave them for you to wear in good health, that they will not be eaten by moths. God knows he would choose for you . . ."

From behind there came a sudden echoed sob. They turned as Pietro ran between them and threw himself against his father's empty clothes. "What will Pappa wear, what will Pappa wear when he comes home?" he cried.

Emilia took him up in her arms. "Signor Mario will only keep them clean and safe from moths till Pappa comes home," she said. "Who would care for them here in this house?"

And though Mario carried him downstairs, promised him a ride in back of the truck, told him of the park and trees near the house he would live in with Zia Emilia and Zia Lenora, Pietro could not be persuaded to stop crying. Finally he fell asleep in the restaurant-keeper's lap sitting in a parlor chair beside the icebox in the open wagon that was to carry them from the past, while upstairs the

114

women wailed against the barren walls of the tenement flat as Emilia swept clean the kitchen floor: "That no word can be said against me," she whispered, "that no word will be said."

"And what was it like in Brooklyn?" Giorgio asked. "I had many friends who lived there years ago."

Pietro shrugged his shoulders. "In Brooklyn you went upstairs to go to bed," he said, "and everyone had his own room." He got up from the rock he was sitting on and drank from the pipe at Christ's feet. He glanced at the statue before returning to his uncle, wiping his mouth dry of the cold water.

"No, I would not be speaking truly if I did not say Brooklyn was good," he admitted quietly. "I too had many friends, and played ball in the street with the stick of a broom. Mario came to see us two or three times a week. Under his direction, we made wine every year."

He paused, considered something, and then went on. "His sister, Lenora, was good with us. She reminded me a little of an older Teresa." Pietro smiled, remembering something special about Lenora. "On Sunday morning, she used to put on a trace of lipstick before she went to Mass."

He shut his eyes and the slow walks home from church drifted back to him, the perfumed stream of women dressed as though for Easter in brilliant coats of yellow and lilac and blue and green—daughters of the Neapolitans born in Brooklyn—and clean-shaved men, their husbands and brothers, every one of them speaking English, for Brooklyn was America as Grand Street had never been. Then they turned off Thirteenth Avenue, away from the air of bottled flowers, and were greeted at every brick-faced house by the crackling odors of chickens roasting, spaghetti sauce simmering, artichokes boiling, peppers frying: a symphony of scents that soon signified Sunday morning as clearly as any calendar.

"Before sitting down to eat," Pietro remembered, "she used to wipe off the lipstick with toilet paper so as not to smear the napkin.

"Then, after eating, those peaceful afternoons, we sat in the parlor and Emilia and Lenora would read aloud from *Il Progresso* for my benefit as well as theirs." He looked away from Giorgio. "The true Italian of the newspaper was supposed to compensate for the dialect we spoke."

Giorgio smiled. "You speak it well."

Pietro nodded. "I remember one of those lessons. It was an article about casualties suffered by the Italian Army in Abyssinia after the war was over. Death from partisan forces, disease, malnutrition."

"The after-effects of every battle," Giorgio said quietly.

"Mario came that afternoon. Zia Emilia was suspicious right away, for he had been to see us just the day before. She knew he would not have returned so soon without good reason—or bad. She should have been a detective."

Mario's face was red as fire from the cold outdoors and his lips chilled Pietro's cheek with their kiss. "Lucky are you to be inside, Pietro mio," Mario said happily. "Many is the frozen nose I stumbled across in the street this ice-cold day." For Mario, summer heat ran a river of perspiration through which one had to wade, and winter's cold caused noses to fall like icicles.

"Is it that cold?" Lenora asked.

"Oh yes, oh yes," Mario said seriously. "Why not?" He took two tiny boxes of torrone candy from his pocket and smuggled them into Pietro's hands. "Do not let them be seen by Zia Emilia," he whispered. "Quickly, hide them away."

"Mario," Emilia said wearily, "it is not necessary to bring him something every time you come."

"Deprive an old man of an innocent pleasure?" He turned to be sure Pietro had run from the room. "Go fry yourself. As for you, sister mine, do I not deserve a cup of coffee?"

"Immediately, your eminence. See with what airs he arrives this day."

Lenora gone to the kitchen, Emilia sought Mario's dark eyes. "Why this visit?" she asked evenly, "what has happened?"

Mario threw up his hand. "Why must I always wait for something to happen before I can allow myself the company of my sister, the smile of my godson, and the good humor of his aunt?" He repeated Emilia's question in her own apprehensive voice. "What's happened? Nothing has happened." Averting her insistent gaze, he took a de Nobili from his pocket and reached for the newspaper.

"We saw each other just yesterday," Emilia reminded him.

Mario nodded, his ragged head lost for an instant in a cloud of smoke impatiently exhaled.

"Mario, look at me. I read you like a book. Do not play the child with me, I beg of you."

"Ooo fa." He turned a few pages of the paper and

then without looking up, said, "Yesterday there came a letter to me from Rome."

The low sound she drew through her lips as she took the envelope from Mario's hand expressed Emilia's end of waiting, release from hope, her recognition as confession whatever words Natale had contrived to write. "What does he say?"

"I do not know," Mario said. "As you see, your letter is sealed. It was addressed to me in an outer envelope along with a note in which he asked me to watch over you and the boy. As though I needed to be asked," he muttered.

With slow hands she slit the envelope and withdrew the letter. A slip of paper fluttered to the floor. It was a bank draft for two hundred dollars. With a sigh, Emilia set it aside on her lap and turned to the ill-spaced lines of her brother's hand.

Mario watched her as she read, expecting, with each tired nod of her head that confirmed her most oppressing fears, an explosion of anger and grief. But she finished the first page in silence, and then the second.

At last she returned the letter, along with the check, to the envelope. She rubbed her eyes with the back of her hands and smiled feebly, accepting the consciousness to which she had been awakened. "He has been knighted by Mussolini to the Order of Annunziata," she said, "and lives in a villa with servants enough for the Pope." She made the Sign of the Cross. "One thing, only one, weighs heavy on his breast—longing for his son. But he will send for us in a matter of months, he says, as soon as he is fully established. Till then," she tapped the envelope lightly, "the money will continue." She closed her eyes

118

and shook her head slowly, murmuring, "Not a word about Sempione, not a word about the devil Rocco."

"Little there is he can say," Mario said.

Emilia opened her eyes. "Look," she said, "it is not necessary for the little one to know of this letter."

"But why?"

"In recent days he has not asked about his father. Better it would be to save it for a time of needed courage." Emilia put the letter in the pocket of her apron. "I for one prefer to remain in America. I like not a bit the turn Italia takes these last few . . ."

She was interrupted by Lenora's entrance with the coffee tray. "Have you been saying your rosary together?" she asked with a laugh.

"The time for prayer has passed," Emilia said.

"And so has it passed for tragedy." Mario took the cup Lenora gave him. He helped himself to two spoons of sugar and stirred his coffee. "I do not say you should sing yourself a song, or dance from room to room. But neither should your spirit be cloaked in black and pounded a mia colpa with closed hand for a political death beyond your control."

"Your speech is like a colander, thoughtfully formed but full of holes."

"Apply your wit to a more happy existence, if not for yourself then for those around you," Mario retorted. He tasted his coffee and added more sugar.

Lenora shook her head and laughed. "May I please know what passes between you now?"

Mario told her about the letter and when he had finished, Lenora nodded and held her hands before her breast in a diminutive gesture of surrender. "I do not defend him," she said, "and I do not say what he did was right. But he did what he thought was right, and so in a way must be admired."

"You are generous to the point of sin," Emilia murmured.

"He could well be remembered as a patriot of Fascist Italy."

Mario turned away slowly. "A dubious honor at best." He put on his coat and kissed his sister and Emilia. "Where is Pietro?"

"Probably with his ear to the radio upstairs."

"Let him be," Mario said. "Arrivederci. We see each other soon."

From his secret place under the dining room table with its crocheted cloth like a tent flap nearly to the floor, the gift of torrone unopened in his hands, Pietro saw the big black shoes pass like freight cars before his wondering eyes.

"And so I learned my father was hailed as a hero by the great Mussolini," Pietro reflected, "and despised by my aunt at the same time. That he would send for us to join him in Italy, and that Zia Emilia did not want to go to him. That he loved me as always and missed me, and that I was not to be told he had written. I did not even understand why he had gone away from us in the first place."

"Did you ever ask?"

"Oh yes. I asked again and again till I tired of the answer I knew even as a child had been invented to quiet my anxieties. I was told Pappa had received a telegram saying his closest friend was dying in Italy, and that

Pappa had gone to him, that he would return as soon as the friend got better—or died."

Pietro laughed aloud at himself, at the outrageousness of the tale, at the gullibility of the boy who had accepted it. "I believed it for a while. But then as the friend continued for months to swing between life and death, the explanation became ludicrous even to the mind of a child. Emilia was stuck with that story and I could never ask again *why* Pappa had left us. The best I could hope for was an answer to the question, When is he coming back.

"Nor was I successful there. One day Emilia would answer, 'The friend is much better, Pappa returns to us soon.' Another time the friend had taken a turn for the worst and was expected to die in a matter of weeks, at which time Pappa would come home.

"Finally my question and Emilia's answers became a game in which I lost interest. Obviously it could be played forever. I stopped asking about Pappa and then I stopped thinking about him too."

Giorgio mumbled to himself.

"Oh, do not worry. I was not permitted to forget him. There was always something—a word, a place, a person—that drew him back to my mind, and the whole thing would start again inside me. I used to torment myself with every aspect of his disappearance, every tiny fact a grain of sand I scraped against my sensibilities till resentment and self-pity formed around me like a cultivated pearl."

Giorgio did not answer, and he did not move. At twenty feet, silhouetted against the pale sky, he could have passed for part of the rock he sat on. He waited for Pietro to continue.

"Not to change the subject—in America during the war, parents of sons drafted into service used to hang a small flag in the window of their home, with a blue star to represent every man in the family under arms. A gold star indicated a death.

"One Saturday afternoon, I found Mario, elbows on the kitchen table, face hidden behind handkerchief, unable to still the sobs that racked his heart. I was afraid to ask what had happened. His son Michele was in the Pacific and nothing had been heard from him in weeks. It was terrible to see Mario cry. At last he took control of himself and shook his head. 'Are these the things they teach you in your school?' he asked me. 'What happened?' I asked.

" 'Do not be afraid, it is nothing. Just that last night they threw a brick through the restaurant window and stole the flag of my son that was hanging there.' He wiped his face with his big bare hand. 'They want to see that star gold before they know how much we suffer with that bastard on the other side,' he said."

Pietro stopped and took out the cigarettes again. "Mario was talking about Mussolini, of course. But for a swift instant, I thought he meant my father."

Giorgio accepted his light and waved the match out with his hand. "Ah, but why? How could your father enter into that act of pigs?"

Pietro nodded. "Because my country was at war with Mussolini. My father had been rewarded by Mussolini for something he had done—what, I did not know at that time. I felt ashamed, as an American and as an Italian. At that moment I could be proud of nothing. In school we bought War Stamps and made posters that ridiculed the Axis. At home we mourned poor Italy as American planes destroyed the land I sprang from. And

122

Emilia crazy without letters from her brother, my father."

Giorgio stopped him. "Now you are going to tell me about the war. The war was here," he reminded Pietro. "You speak of shame, the Germans destroying us more cruelly than your bombers. Our sons and grandsons in American uniforms fighting against . . ." He stopped himself. "A hundred years have passed," he said quietly. "That it be forgotten."

Pietro nodded. "How we celebrated the Armistice. Churchbells sang and sirens screamed and the horns of automobiles were sounded in the street where Mario roamed with a gallon under his arm, stopping strangers and making them drink to the imminent return of his son from Okinawa."

Giorgio smiled and rubbed his arms free of the goosepimples that had risen under his skin in memory of those sad jubilant days.

"We made wine for the first time since the beginning of the war," Pietro said. "Emilia, Lenora, Teresa, Serafina, Luigi, Mario, and I made wine. Mario took me with him to buy the grapes. I remember we rode on the Thirteenth Avenue trolley car far downtown, far beyond a point where the tracks crossed under the elevated line, through the Jewish section where old men with curled white beards sat like statues in sunny squares of sidewalk before a synagogue with magic numbers in the window, to a place where a single freight car had come to a dead stop on deserted rails."

There was a ladder that climbed from the weeds to the car's high barn doors, to the splintered steel-laced floors and the cases of grapes stacked eight feet to the ceiling along the walls and the sweet sticky smell of fruit.

A squat man in a pea coat perched atop a throne of boxes in a corner watched Mario and Pietro climb into the car. He did not move and they didn't see him there in the half light. He watched Mario help himself to a few handfuls of grapes which he shared with the boy and then he jumped down to the floor. "Cumpa," he grumbled, "are you going to make wine or did you just stop in for a banquet?"

Mario turned quickly. "Whey Cumpa," he said, "not bad this year, is it?"

The squat man lit the toscano which he produced from his pocket. "You know good grapes when you taste them, brother mine. You have been eating from a seven-dollar case."

Mario laughed. "Take two handfuls from the ones I buy."

The man smiled and nodded. "How does it go?" he asked gently.

"Without pain," Mario answered. He put his arm around Pietro's shoulder and pushed him forward. "Cumpa, this is my godson," he said, and in his enthusiasm to get a good price on the grapes, added, "If I am not mistaken, you used to know his father."

The squat man chewed his cigar and spat on the floor. "Who was that?"

Mario took a single black grape and polished it with his fingers till it shone like marble. He held it up to the light of the doorway and pretended to look through it as though it had been a glass of wine. "Ah, what color," he said, and kissed the grape.

"Who was the father?" the man in the pea coat asked again.

"Natale Sbagliato, Don Natale. You worked for him

years ago," Mario answered. He popped the grape into his mouth and turned to the cases piled along the walls of the freight car. "Let us see what could make a good wine to celebrate the end of the war," he said, and winked at Pietro, and the boy smiled.

The squat man took the cigar out of his mouth and turned to Pietro. "You are the son of Natale Sbagliato?"

Pietro nodded his head a little, afraid the man would throw them out.

"Take some more grapes, sonny," he said in English, "your father's a prince, I swear to God," and he raised his right hand, stained purple, above his shoulder.

Mario called from a case he was examining, "What do we have here, Cumpare? What do we need for a beautiful red wine?"

"You know better than I what is needed," the man answered, and then looked at Pietro. "I used to drive a truck for your father years ago, sonny," he said in English again. "Those were the days." He turned and spoke in Italian to Mario. "Do you remember Rocco Gargatto? That poor cracked ass. Nice and fat had he gotten in America, and then to allow that big-titted whore to put fire to his pants."

Mario nodded toward Pietro. "He understands Italian," he said evenly.

"And what do I say?" the squat man demanded. "What the devil." He smiled and showed round stumps of teeth. "Without the war, Rocco would have found himself in Paradise over there, eh? Who knows what became of him? Do you ever hear a word from him, Cumpa?"

"No."

"And how's your father doin' these days, sonny? Where's he at now?"

Pietro shook his head. He felt a sudden nausea rise

through his stomach and he swallowed hard because he was afraid he was going to be sick. His mouth dried and he felt perspiration on his forehead.

"Hey, what is it?" The squat man took the toscano from his mouth and called to Mario. "Cumpa, what is it with this one?"

Mario helped him down the ladder into the bright sun of the October morning. "The smell of all that grape," he said softly. "I too felt like fainting." He stayed with Pietro for ten minutes and then climbed back up into the freight car.

Pietro sat down on a dead rail. The weeds were over his head. From the freight car came the buzz of Mario's whisper, sharp, urgent. Then the grape man said defensively, "Cumpa, what do you want of me? You are the one who spoke first of Natale Sbagliato."

Mario's whisper, like a saw through hard wood.

And then the other, disgustedly, "Better to keep him in a cage of glass, Cumpa. Close him up in a monastery."

Mario's whisper was more gentle this time, and when the grape man answered his tone was apologetic. Pietro could not hear what was said. He got up from the rail and walked closer to the freight car. They were talking about the grapes.

". . . a few cases of Zinfandel, one or two white Malaga for coloration and bouquet, if you desire, one of raisins for extra spirit," the squat man was saying, "and you get a wine fit for a sky-blue God. Listen to what I say, Cumpa. I'll give you a special price. In memory of other times, am I understood? And truly, I am sorry about the boy."

Mario sighed. "I am sorry, too."

In a little while, Mario came down the ladder. When he caught Pietro's eyes he smiled. "It is going to be the

126

finest wine we ever made," he said. He patted Pietro's shoulder lightly. "How do you feel now?" he asked.

"Okay."

Mario said nothing more about the grape man's questions or Pietro's reaction to them. As they walked back toward the trolley stop, Pietro started to say something but then checked himself. Mario glanced at him once, afraid to open his mouth, that it might be misinterpreted as encouragement for questions.

And so did Pietro remain silent. He shut his mind to the implications of the grape man's words. Whatever it was that was being kept from him, it loomed ahead like a school examination for which he was ill-prepared, for which he could not prepare. He preferred not to think about it. Pappa was in Italy at the side of a dying friend. That was all he was to know.

Mario worked him hard when the grapes were delivered. There were thirty-six cases to be carried to the cellar. "Eighteen for you, eighteen for me," Mario said. Thirty-two pounds at a time and after four trips it was the weight of the world. The rough wood splintered the inside of his fingers and his arms trembled with fatigue. He stopped counting after ten trips and continued like a machine to haul the crates away, smiling at Mario with toscano between clenched teeth as they passed one another in the backyard. Once, twice, Mario suggested he stop to rest but Pietro did not stop. Just before lunch, Zia Emilia looked through the kitchen window and cried out at the sight of him stumbling up from the cellar, his back frozen in an arch, his face flushed, his mouth open and dry.

She ran out and swung Pietro's arms away from the boxes. "That you are thrown behind bars," she cried at Mario. "The stevedore torture you put him to."

Mario glanced at the remaining boxes of grapes. "Three more cases and he has carried off his half of the work."

"The soul of God is a baby . . ."

"And so will he remain with only women about him. Now go, before you yourself are made to carry down the rest." He winked at Pietro who cradled those last three cases in his arms, one by one, as though they were flesh and blood he hauled to Paradise.

Then he locked himself in the bathroom till his breathing returned to normal and he was able to hide the trembling of his arms by keeping his hands in his pockets. He rolled up his sleeves and made a muscle which he tested with sore fingers. He combed his dark hair and gazed at himself in the mirror over the sink.

Later, they set two open-head barrels up on boxes twelve inches off the floor so that the following week, when the bubbling grape juice was ready to be drawn off and stored for aging in the master barrel, the bung would be in position to be replaced by the tap. Then they set the masher atop number one and opened the first cases of grapes. Pietro stood on a chair and emptied the first half case into the hopper and Mario turned the handle, the crushed pulp and stems and streaming juice running into the barrel like an echoing rain.

Lenora came downstairs with two gallon jugs of old wine. Zia Emilia followed behind her with four glasses. The handle of the masher turning creaked and the juices poured into the barrel. Lenora cracked the sealing wax from the first jug. "It is the last the good soul of my husband made himself." Mario quit work and Pietro stepped down from the chair. Lenora poured the wine.

"A little water in it, Pietro," Emilia said as she handed him his glass.

128

"Leave him alone," Mario commanded. "You would teach him to piss in this barrel." Mario carried his glass to the door and held it to the sun. "It has good color." Then he came back and they clinked four glasses and they drank to the memory of Lenora's husband, who had made the wine, and to the end of the war.

"I would be content with a wine half as good as this one," Mario said as he smacked his lips. He poured the rest of his glass into the barrel, for luck. Lenora filled his glass again and when the women had gone upstairs, Mario filled Pietro's glass. "So you know what it is you make," he said. And they set again to work.

The others came before the barrel was half full—Teresa, Serafina, and Luigi. Pietro tried hard to keep his eyes from slipping below Teresa's neck. His hand trembled as he drank the good sour wine as he worked, and at last he gazed shamelessly at those great breasts that seemed about to burst the cloth that held them. They cried out to him and his insides weakened.

"Pietro, dear one." She hugged him and kissed his face and pulled his hair roughly. "What does it seem to you, this wine-making of America, eh?" she laughed. "In the old country, off with the shoes and tratta tra, tratta tra"—she jumped up and down, holding him fast—"we used to dance the grapes into wine. But what am I doing?" she cried and held him away, "I treat you still as a child. Go, go back to man's work." She went to Mario and slapped his back. "Mario, I came to work. What can I do? Let me turn the handle a little."

"Teresa beautiful, you turn my handle every time I look at you."

Her eyes laughed at him over the rim of the glass she drank from.

"Pietro, show her how to open the boxes," Mario

said; then to the barber, "Luigi, if you can risk the danger of stained hands, throw more grapes here, that this wine-making begins to take form."

Teresa stood close, watching him as he forced the big screwdriver under the lid and pried open the box, and when she leaned forward to take it from his hand, her breasts cushioned his elbow and he quickly straightened his arm as though he'd been caught stealing.

He showed her how to break up the boxes without cracking the wood, so it could be used for something other than burning, and how to retrieve the nails without bending them. He stared as she hammered apart a crate, and when she splintered the second side and glanced up at him to apologize for her clumsiness, he said quietly, "It does not matter."

Teresa lowered her eyes to her work. "Help them make the wine," she whispered gently, "that you are no longer a child."

When they had finished squeezing the grapes, and they had eaten, Mario took down his guitar and made Pietro dance the tarantella with Teresa. The guitar sent him round and round the cellar room, holding tight to Teresa's hands, his arms out straight. Then bang together as she hooked his arm and held it firm with his elbow against her breast, her face in a fun house laugh, her hair bouncing bouncing about her shoulders, the others laughing and clapping tarantella tarantella la la lala la la la la, teen ti teenti teen ti teenti tarantella tarantell', faster, faster, and they stamped their feet and the guitar got lost and they danced and danced till Teresa caught him in both her arms and hugged him till they stopped, stumbling still after the guitar had finished, unable to keep their balance after the dizzying whirl, his hands on her soft hot hips as he fought to steady himself, unable to focus, Teresa screaming with laughter and joy.

Then the guitar started again and Luigi danced with Zia Emilia and Lenora at the same time, one on each arm, and then the women began to perspire and tire and the tarantella turned into war marches because now the war was over, and the choruses were shrill and thin, played on a guitar and sung by two men and three women with knowledge that the Fascist dream that had inspired *Giovinezza*, youth, springtime of eternal beauty, had ended in a nightmare.

They stopped singing and Mario picked out on a single string the melody of *Facetta Nera*, little black face of Abyssinia, and played it as if on the mandolin, his right hand trembling over the mouth of the guitar like the wings of a hummingbird at a deep dark flower. When the fragile march was over, Luigi sighed and spoke its final line. *"Viv' il Duce, e Viv' il Re,"* he said and shook his head.

Zia Emilia cried in silence, the tears rolling slowly down her cheeks and no one said anything, and the guitar was still and they waited; and then Pietro saw her and went to her and she took his hands and tried to stop the tears and she began to smile. But when Luigi said softly, "Emilia, you must not cry before this boy, what is done is done," her strength gave way and she screamed in a way that shot a chill through Pietro's chest and she held him and moaned, "If only I were the only one who would ever know the meaning of these tears."


Pietro cleared his throat. "She was crying for my father," he said to Giorgio, "and for me, his fatherless son. Teresa and Lenora took her upstairs and in a little while all the wine I had drunk suddenly reached my head and I went to bed." Pietro smiled sadly. "A few days later, I found all the letters my father had written, neatly tied and hidden away in Emilia's closet."

Giorgio cracked the thick knuckles of his hands. "But you had known there were letters," he said.

Pietro shook his head.

"You have just finished telling me of that first letter Mario took to Emilia in Brooklyn," Giorgio reminded him.

"That was seven years before," Pietro said. "In those seven years, I had succeeded in forgetting it. As far as I was concerned, no letters existed. After all, of what use could they have been to me, when I was to know only what I was told?"

Giorgio agreed. "But how did you come to find them?" he asked.

"One day I returned home from school and found a note from Zia Emilia asking me to go buy bread. She and Lenora had gone to pick up more embroidery work, but they had forgotten to leave money for the bread.

"Now Emilia used to keep loose change in an empty chocolate box in the first drawer of her bureau. That day, the box was empty. I looked in the second drawer. Nothing."

In the bottom drawer he discovered a cache of extravagant nightgowns and slips of lace and ribbon, delicately monogrammed ES above the heart, white turned pale yellow with age, the dim scent of lilac a fading hope that this, Emilia's trousseau, would ever be put into use. Pietro touched the soft heavy silk, and sorrow drifted through him with the realization that Zia Emilia, an old woman who wore always the same tattered housedress

132

and plain underclothes he'd seen on the line, had a drawer full of riches that had lost all value waiting for a wedding night fated never to come.

In the bottom of her closet he found a cardboard carton hidden behind the hem of old coats and dresses. It was filled with letters tied together with red and yellow embroidery thread. The first letter he read told of the May Day celebration the day before in the village of Masinalto by partisan elements who had slipped red ribbons around the barrels of their submachine guns and dropped all pretense of being anything but Communist. In the piazza they had constructed two rag dummies representing Mussolini and Clara Petacci, and had hung them upside down in the doorway of a suspected Fascist sympathizer whom they had executed the preceding day before the eyes of his wife and twelve-year-old son.

*Ironically I am well regarded because of my separation from my family who live in America, and because I know a little English. The past few months I have been employed by the local Allied Military Government as translator of civilian orders. All in all I pass it well, though tortured always by my longing to see you and that beloved soul of God my son. Hold him close to you, Emilia, that he grows honest and true beyond my life. Regards to those who still remember me, I hold you embraced to my heart and kiss your cheek, affectionately as always, your brother,*

*Natale.*

Pietro lowered the letter to the pile he had taken it from. For an instant he fought the sob that rose in his throat, and then he let it burst, and he cried aloud.

Zia Emilia was in the doorway. "You have found them," she said simply.

He looked up. "Why did you never tell me about them, why were they hidden from me?" Pietro demanded.

"You were too young to understand." Zia Emilia sat down on the bed. She saw the drawers of the bureau, imperfectly shut. "How did you know to look for them?"

"I did not know. I looked for money for the bread. How was I too young to understand that my father sends his love to me and I am never told?"

Emilia went to his side and examined the bundles of letters. "You have read them all?" she asked.

He shook his head. "Just this one."

She took it from his hand and read it through quickly, having forgotten it. It was innocent. The pounding about her heart quieted and she offered an inaudible prayer of thanks to God. "You knew he was in Italy," she said quietly. "He went there years ago when you were very young. Little by little, memory of him disappeared from your head. It was better for you to forget him than to live in sorry longing for him. Mario has been your father in his place."

"But why the secrets, the letters tied and hidden in back of your closet all these years?" Pietro insisted.

Emilia sighed. "When you are older you will better understand the mistaken steps the best of men in good faith stumble into. Your father's love for you was matched only by his love for the country of his birth, and his desire for you to attain someday a position of respect was matched by his desire for Italy to attain a position of respect now, in his lifetime.

"One day he received a letter from the man who had called him to this country in the first place, a man called Rocco Gargatto. Rocco had returned to the other side with sympathy and enthusiasm for Mussolini. I speak now of depression days," Emilia said and she rubbed her stomach to indicate food had been scarce. "He promised your father a job in the government with good pay, just as he had promised him a place with the railroad in Oregon years before. You remember stories Pappa used to tell of that work out west?"

Pietro nodded his head slowly, the subject of trains and shovels and mountains a familiar one from somewhere in the past.

Emilia continued her story, improvising here, elaborating there till the net effect of the tale she wove amounted to Natale's decision to return to Italy and high-paying employment, thus serving both the country of his birth and his family in New York. "His plan was to call us to him and we would all live in a villa like the royal family," she said.

"America was not at war with Italy at that time, so your father went not against the country of your birth. But then the war began, and he found himself allied to both sides, though bound to Italy by his presence there. Remember that every Italian in America had relatives on the other side—brothers, cousins, uncles, nephews—flesh and blood that became our enemy, just as we became theirs, through the will of a lunatic. But to leave the country would have been an act of treason. When the Ar-

135

mistice was signed, your father joined the Allies and as you just read works now as translator in Masinalto, where we were born."

Emilia turned away, afraid he had sensed her fabrication. She glanced at the Sacred Heart above her bed and asked forgiveness.


Giorgio picked up the pack of cigarettes Pietro had set down on the rock beside him. "First the unhappy memory of making wine, then the unhappy memory of buying bread." He accepted Pietro's light. "You recite a Mass of misery for yourself. Is it possible no pleasant thoughts have stayed with you from your days of youth?" Giorgio smiled suddenly. "Listen to me, speaking of your youth as though you were my age now. Your cynicism must be a contagious one."

"You asked to be told of those things related to a father's disappearance."

"Very well. Now temper your story with the memory of something good."

Pietro shrugged his shoulders. He reached back and remembered. "The first time I made love."

"Ah."

"I was prohibited to see this girl. Zia Emilia considered her too much woman for her age. She was called Virginia and at sixteen years enjoyed the admiration of grown men." Pietro shut his eyes, thought of the time he told her her tits were like a quart-and-a-half of ice cream packed into quart containers, and she had kissed him and asked what flavor. He remembered her as vanilla-fudge in the summer, her smooth skin brown where the sun reached her, and where it did not she remained pale as a nun. She wore her black hair braided, then ringed round

136

her head like the crown of a gypsy queen. Undone, it tumbled to her waist. Her Sicilian blood showed in her full lips and magic eyes, and there was a time when just a look from her excited him more than another's embrace. She had a lovely face and in the darkness of a Sunday afternoon in the last row of the Endicott Theatre her thighs were warm as naptime milk.

"We had gone to the Festa of the Assumption in back of Saint Bernadette's in Brooklyn," Pietro said, and the wet smell of the summer's grass trampled into the sand came back to him, and he smiled again as he remembered that long-ago night.

She had taken him by the arm and directed him to one of the booths, whispering, "Get me a tiger, Pete, get me a tiger." With three successive balls he banged off a pyramid of wooden blocks and she had her tiger. She kissed him for it, reminding him that Zia Emilia and Lenora and everyone else was at home, that there was no one at the Festa to police his behavior.

"I'm going to win a bottle of whiskey," he said and kept her at his elbow as dime by dime he lost a dollar thirty on the numbered oilcloth strip waiting for 24—Virginia's birthday in February—to be stopped on green by the clothespin clattering against the spinning wheel. The next dime won, and he chose a pint of Three Feathers.

"You can have a big bottle, dumbbell," one of the losers said, and the man running the booth put a hand on a fifth and waited.

"The little one," Pietro said again, and as they hurried away, the pint already out of sight in his pocket, his arm around his girl, explained, "What the hell would we do with the big one? We'd only waste it."

They bought two bottles of cold ginger ale on the

way to the park, and with his last half-dollar, cigarettes from Mr. Aderman who had them for sale throughout the war at fifty cents a pack.

In two blocks they had passed the rim of the Festa's light and confusion and walked slowly hand in hand under the canopy of cool dark leaves spread by trees that grew at the edge of the street, accompanied all the way by the theme of *Madame Butterfly*, which drifted high above them from the bandstand behind the church.

They strolled through the park's paths of luminescent gravel, past the swings and monkey bars to the playing fields beyond, and lay at last in one another's arms in darkness of the infield grass, listening for a trumpet phrase as they urged on the joy of their love.

"Let's stop for a while," Virginia whispered, out of breath. "Let's have a drink and a cigarette."

"We forgot to bring cups." He unscrewed the cap and tilted the bottle hesitantly to his lips.

"How's it taste?"

"Awful."

She giggled softly. "What are we going to do?"

He found his penknife and pried out the bottle-opener blade. "We'll drink some of the ginger ale plain and then pour this stuff in and drink from the bottle."

They would not admit it did not taste good but they had come this far and they would drink it. They shared two cigarettes and finished the first bottle of ginger ale and whisky, and lay down again. Virginia took her blouse off altogether at last and Pietro with trembling fingers undid the tight strap at her back and she came free with a sigh.

She let him kiss her breasts and bury his face there and with a smile on her lips she undid his trousers.

He remembered a red balloon high above his head and the next morning too, the air half gone, how it had been soft and wrinkly in his hand. It was another Festa in another land, a land of children and fathers hand in hand, where you were carried to bed and kissed in your sleep. He remembered Pappa coming home late that night; no, not coming at all, Zia Emilia screaming and pulling at her hair. And a silver gun in a velvet case held by a big one who spoke no Italian. There was a staircase with people crying out to him, and a scraped knee, just as his elbow burned now against the earth, and a policeman who would not let him pass as he called out to Zia Emilia's screams, Pappa, Pappa.

Pappa: Father.

How strange it was to discover you had a real father far away who wrote letters and who had seen the war and who loved and worried about you. It was a little like discovering you had a second arm after having mastered life with one. One day, maybe, they would be together.

"Faster, Pete, faster," Virginia murmured, and he did, deeper and faster with eyes closed in darkness till the world was lost and the band stopped playing.

When he got home, the house was dark and still except for the kitchen. Zia Emilia met him there, and stopped him. "Where have you been till now?" she demanded, "the hour past midnight? Answer me, your face red with lipstick and humiliation."

"Leave me alone," he said in English. "I'm going to bed."

She stepped before him. "Answer me." Her hand was fast from her bathrobe pocket and slapped him. "You were with that child whore of the snake eyes," she

139

cried. "This hand you will taste so long as I have strength to raise it and you lack sense enough to merit it. Like a storm you carry me back to a long-ago night of worry. You stink of drink," she screamed. "Animal, animal."

Lenora came halfway down the stairs. "What happens?" she whispered, terrified from her sleep.

"Wait, just wait what happens when Mario learns of this night."

"What the hell do I care about Mario," he shouted. He pushed his way past Lenora on the stairs and slammed his door so hard, the calendar of Saint Anthony, patron of orphans, placed on his bedside table three years before by Emilia, fell face down on the floor. He found it there in the morning and hid it in his underwear drawer.

"You took this girl to the Festa of the Assumption in back of the church," Giorgio prompted, "and then—?"

Pietro nodded his head and smiled. "And then we made love in a park nearby."

Giorgio looked away and sighed. "I too remember the first time I made love," he said wistfully. "Ah. And the girl? Did you continue to see her?" he asked. "She sounds like a joy."

"Yes, I continued to see her," Pietro said, "until I went away to the university."

"It was far from her?"

"No, not too far, but far enough so that I lived away from home."

"And Zia Emilia permitted it?"

"Three hours a day of train was too much even for her to allow."

"Her pride at seeing you at the university justified your absence, of that I am certain," Giorgio said. "I too have pride in you, that you are the son of my brother and that you have been to the university."

"Pride in me," Pietro muttered in English.

"Eh?"

"Nothing," Pietro said, "nothing. Tell me, have you ever seen a university?"

"I? Never. Where would I see one? In Masinalto?"

Pietro smiled. "Did you know there are entire buildings filled with books?"

"Of course. The library. Certain things even I know."

"And did you know certain libraries have the newspapers of every day, going back as far as fifty years?"

"This I did not know."

"Nor did I know before I went to the university."

"Every day for fifty years! Truly? There must be newspapers like this." Giorgio raised his eyes to the sky, to indicate the stack of newspapers fifty years would build.

Pietro shook his head. "No. They make photographs of every page of the newspapers and reduce them to the size of a postage stamp. When you want to read them, you pass them through a machine that enlarges them on a screen, like the film of a motion picture."

"What a fine way to read the newspaper," Giorgio cried. "What a fine way to attend the university. Bravo, Professore."

"I will never forget the first time I read a newspaper in that fashion," Pietro said quietly.

Giorgio looked at him closely. "What was it you read, that it stays with you this way?" he asked.

Pietro rested his head in his hands, as though the memory of that article wearied him. "Five lines about Rocco Gargatto," he said.

"Ah." The sound was a delicate moan. "And one newspaper led to another."

"Exactly."

The librarian helped him thread the microfilm on the projector, and showed him how to advance the pages by turning the knob on the side of the machine. Then she glanced at the big clock on the wall behind her desk and said, "You don't have much time. We close at ten. It's a quarter of now."

Pietro nodded. "I just want to check something. It'll take me a minute." He gazed down at the projected image of the front page. STRIKE ON BUSES SET FOR TOMORROW. He turned the knob and watched the pages roll past. Page thirty-three . . . column five. There!

The brief article describing a reading by Dylan Thomas told him nothing he hadn't already known. He glanced at his watch. Ten minutes to kill. "At least I learned to work this thing," he thought, and his eyes darted about the pages he slid before them.

They froze on a headline on the last page.

## 10 ARRESTED HERE
## IN NARCOTICS RING

Former Lieutenant of Rocco Gargatto
Among Those Held in High Bail

142

"Rocco Gargatto." The name knifed through his memory and came to rest on his father's lips. Rocco Gargatto was the one who had sent for him in Italy and paid for his passage to the railroad gang in Oregon; Rocco Gargatto was the one who had rescued him in the mountain cave-in; Rocco Gargatto was the one who had set him up in the grocery business; Rocco Gargatto was the one Pappa and Zia Emilia used to fight about years ago.

The article told of the arrest by Federal agents of top racketeers charged with conspiracy to violate the narcotics laws in connection with a delivery of heroin on August 10, 1947, at Forty-second Street and Pershing Square. It gave the names, ages, and addresses of those taken. They were all Italian, Pietro realized with a chill, with the single exception of a Jew, and a new paragraph began:

> Held in $50,000 bail was Onofrio (Fat Freddy) Ravino, 57, of 1123 Bay Parkway, Brooklyn, an intimate of underworld figures and long-time lieutenant of Rocco Gargatto. Gargatto, 62, a fugitive from justice, is wanted on charges of extortion, conspiracy, smuggling, and for the brutal murder of a call girl sweetheart who turned state's evidence against him in connection with a Mann Act violation in 1933.

> He escaped to Italy 17 years ago and is believed to be a master planner of an international narcotics ring currently operating out of Naples.

143

This was Rocco Gargatto. This was the man his father swore by, as other men swear by Christ. Pietro read the paragraph again, and then a third time, and still he was unable to roll the page away from sight. He heard the librarian call, "We're closing up now," and he didn't move. He wasn't thinking about Rocco Gargatto, or his father either. What held him fixed in place was the fortuitous way in which this information had come to him.

The librarian touched his shoulder. "Closing time."

Pietro stood up. He rewound the microfilm and returned the spool to its box. The librarian took it and returned it to the stacks. It might not be called for again for five years.

Truth kicked him in the throat. Pappa had lied to him, had created a fabric of lies about Rocco Gargatto, and passed off those inventions as truth to the ingenuous mind of a child. Why?

He left the library confused, certain the information he had inadvertently gathered was related somehow to his father's disappearance, but he did not know how. He considered telephoning Zia Emilia but decided against it. She would only be disturbed that he had learned the truth about Rocco, and would not contribute anything to it. Then he thought of Mario. He would be able to push Mario.

He hurried down One Hundred Fourteenth Street, past the brownstone building that housed his basement furnished room, to Broadway and then over two blocks to the subway.

The station platform was deserted and he lit a cigarette for company against the dank urine smell and dim light of underground. He went to the very edge of the platform and peered down the black tunnel. A single

144

headlight signaled the faraway approach of his train. He watched the headlight grow as the train hurtled toward him, and suddenly a fear mounted harder and harder against his stomach, an indeterminate fear that banged into focus and was recognized by him as the possibility that Pappa had always worked for Rocco in some capacity against the law; that he had gone to Italy three years after Rocco's escape there to join him in the operation of the narcotics ring described in the article he had just read. It explained both Pappa's lies and his disappearance fourteen years before.

The train was crashing into the station now. He stepped back. The train rushed by and began its brake. The cigarette dropped from Pietro's fingers. The doors opened before him and he stepped into the gritty train. The doors closed and the train began to move again.

# CHAPTER 7

THE LIGHTS IN THE WINDOW of Cafe Mario were out, but the place was not closed. Pietro saw Mario at the cash register, his back to the street, counting the day's receipts. He rattled the door and the sound made Mario spin around, his eyes opened wide with surprise and fear. Pietro tapped on the glass, and watched Mario come toward him, peering toward the darkness outside in an attempt to see who was at the door.

"Mario, it is I," Pietro called.

Mario's face broke into a laugh and he hurried to open up. "Whey, what a surprise." He took Pietro's hand with both of his and kissed his mouth.

"How does it go, Mario?"

"Not bad for an old man."

"I am sorry I come at so late an hour," Pietro said.

Mario disregarded his apology. "Let me look at you, godson mine," he said, and pulled the string over his head, turning on the ceiling lights. "Eh, a little thin, a little pale. The studies keep you away from bed, it can be seen. Sit down, sit down. A cup of coffee, eh, and a nice piece of pastry. What tastes good to you, Pietro? 'No cannollo, 'na sfogliatella?"

"Grazi, Mario. Nothing. I just wanted to ask you something."

"What do you mean, nothing? You take the train to come see me and I would let you leave with an empty stomach? Maybe you are hungry. A sandwich, a plate of spaghetti?"

Pietro smiled and pulled a chair away from one of the marble-topped tables along the wall. "Just coffee then, if you keep me company."

"Ma shoo I keep you company, and what do you think?"

Pietro sat down. He had come to see the old man in desperation, but the desperation had disappeared and been replaced by sympathy and sorrow for the embarrassment his questions would certainly cause.

He watched Mario draw the first cup of espresso from the coffee maker behind the counter and when the hissing of the steam pressure stopped, called out, "Mario, who is Rocco Gargatto?" his heart beating hard as he gazed at the cafe-keeper's face for a change of expression.

Mario's eyebrows scarcely went up. "There is a name from the past," he said with a smile. He drew off the second coffee and carried the two cups to Pietro's table and sat down. "What makes you ask about Rocco Gargatto at this time?"

"I have my reasons. Please. Who is he?"

Mario dried his hands on his apron and poured sugar into his coffee. "He was an old friend of mine, and of your father," he said quietly.

"Did you know he is wanted by the police?"

Mario smiled. "Everybody is wanted by the police. I

bought black market sugar during the war. What are you trying to say, Pietro?"

"That Rocco Gargatto is wanted for extortion, conspiracy, smuggling, and murder," Pietro said angrily.

Mario slowly nodded his head.

"Did my father ever work for him?" Pietro's voice trembled.

Mario's smile began to fade, but he continued to nod his head and softly said, "And so did I. We all made a little wine and sold it, which was against the law."

Pietro tapped his spoon impatiently against the side of his cup. "That is not the worst of it," he said in little more than a whisper.

"Do you want to hear the very worst thing I know for certain about your father?" Mario demanded. "Is that what you want to hear?"

"I know what it is now," Pietro said. "I read a newspaper of years ago tonight."

Mario did not answer. He lowered his eyes and stirred his coffee and at last murmured, "Then you know."

"Pappa is in Italy, yes, but not at the bedside of a sick friend these fourteen years. All of you have lied to me forever."

"For your own good," Mario said, "you were so young. What would have been the good of . . ."

"You speak to me of wine illegally made and sold. All right, that was against the law but you hurt no one. Justify to me now my father's *present* trade, his partnership with that bastard Rocco and the poisonous drugs they ship like salt to destroy . . ."

Mario looked up and tapped Pietro's hand. "Wait.

149

Wait a minute," he said. He touched Pietro's face. "What are you talking about?"

Pietro freed himself of the caress. "What am I talking about," he said with exaggerated innocence. "I told you I know. I *know*."

Mario screwed up his face and waved his hand before him. "What do you know? What are you saying?"

"I tell you I read about the narcotics ring in Naples," Pietro shouted. "Do you still take me for a child?"

Mario threw back his head and slapped his forehead with the palm of his hand. He began to laugh.

"And what is so funny?"

"Narcotics ring." Mario wiped his face with his hands and the laughter was gone. "Excuse me. I know now the newspaper you read. It was shown to me by a man who was with Rocco when he died—seven years ago."

"He's dead?" Pietro asked incredulously. "But the newspaper . . ."

"That it teaches you a lesson not to believe all you read. Rocco Gargatto was killed in a bombing of Milan by British planes in '43. For some reason the police of this city have it in their heads that he is a capo mafioso in Naples. Yes, yes, with the drugs. They think of him as another Luciano."

"Then Papa is not involved with narcotics?" Pietro asked.

Mario shook his head. "Your poor father. No, he is not involved with the narcotics," he said gently. "Is that what you thought?"

"What was I to think when I saw the article in the newspaper?" Pietro asked. "His disappearance has never been explained to me . . ."

150

Mario inhaled deeply. "And I thought somehow you had learned about the money stolen from the railroad thirty years ago," he said with a sigh.

"What money stolen?"

"You will see its insignificance compared to the crimes you had tonight ascribed to your father," Mario said.

"What money stolen?" Pietro demanded again. The relief he had experienced seconds before concerning his father's innocence was threatened again, this time by someone who knew Pappa, someone Pietro trusted.

"Compared to the narcotics it will seem like the act of a child taking two cents from the paper stand," Mario said soothingly.

"Tell me," Pietro demanded.

Slowly, softly, as though reciting a fairy tale to a child about to be put to bed, Mario told him of the explosion of the mountain shortly after Natale's arrival in Oregon to work on the railroad, about the payroll safe urged open by Rocco's sensitive fingers. Mario shut his eyes. "They took three thousand dollars."

Pietro supported his head with the heel of his hand, his elbow on the table. "They stole the money," he said wearily.

"Those times were desperate, Pietro mine," Mario said. "I say that not to excuse them but to help explain. The company was run by the loudmouth Irish. What can I tell you? Your father confided in me. You are no longer a child."

Pietro nodded his head against his hands.

Mario's gentle voice continued the story of Rocco Gargatto and carried it through the beginning of the Prohibition years.

"First robbery, then bootlegging," Pietro said almost in a whisper, thinking of his father, for the history was his as well as Rocco's. The weight of all he had learned that night tired him and he wished he were asleep somewhere far from the responsibilities he felt forming about him, responsibilities that included the justification of his father's life and abdication of family, and the redemption of his own past years of ignorance.

Mario patted his hand affectionately and smiled, as though reading his mind. "Bootlegging was not a sin in the heart of many of us in those days," he said. "How little it taxed the conscience of an honest man. In the old country, knowledge of fermentation and distillation came with a boy's first kiss and emerged a skill with age. October days, the ankles and wrists of every boy over twelve were stained purple like blood with the pulp and the juice from the wine. Every morning breath bore the whisper of the grape. Many times, through barter or exchange, wine became bread. And each year, the finest wine was set aside for the village priest and drunk in celebration of the Nativity and the Resurrection. It is the body and blood.

"And the Americans passed a law." Mario nodded his head. "That law became the rules of a game to be broken. It was a very profitable game for Rocco Gargatto. He was not all bad, that one. He was a friend of your father, which counts for much. Then, he gave thirty thousand dollars to Mussolini, a good thing at that time. And thousands for new schools, for the Church. He gave everybody a job, and the old people on the other side lived on the money Rocco paid their sons."

Rocco's history continued to flow from Mario's lips and finally, with his extortion of money from enemies of Mussolini illegally in America, and the account of the naked whore thrown dead into the snow in front of the Centre Street Courthouse, Rocco appeared before Pietro's eyes a form part saint, part devil.

Mario finished his coffee. "I repeat to you," he said, and put his hand out before him, palm down, "on the head of my children: your father's association with him included only the whiskey and the wine. Nothing else." Mario lowered his hand. "That is Rocco Gargatto," he said. "He went away when you were an infant and not a word was heard from him again. I told you how I learned of his death."

"How about Pappa? *He* heard from Rocco, didn't he?" Pietro asked. He got up from the table.

"Your father?"

"The letter in which Rocco asked him to go to Italy for a job? You know the one. Emilia told me about it." Pietro gently touched Mario's shoulder.

"Ah," the old man stuttered, "the letter in which . . ."

"Ah," Pietro repeated, and he smiled sadly. "You keep it up about that letter and my father," he said in English.

"What do you say?" Mario said angrily. "If we tell you that is the way . . ."

Pietro kissed him on the cheek. "Grazi, Mario," he said. "I believe you Pappa has nothing to do with the narcotics. But now that I have learned about these old newspapers . . ."

Mario threw up his hands. "Go fry yourself in old newspapers," he cried. "Give me this pleasure—leave old newspapers to those who wrap fish in them, that they stink."


The bells of the Broadway church were chiming midnight when Pietro got back uptown, but instead of going to bed he went to the Hotel Royale and sat at one of the back tables in the bar and with the help of a cold bottle of beer considered the significance of what he had learned from the newspaper and from Mario, his father's protector.

That his father had been a lottery collector had always been part of his unconscious recollection. But at that time, at that place, the occupation had not been a dishonorable one; to have been apprehended on that score in those days was little worse than getting a speeding ticket today, and there was something vaguely romantic about both those infractions of the law.

Then Pappa disappeared. The police came to the house in search of him. For fourteen years, the reason for his disappearance is kept secret. Then tonight, it turns out that his best friend, a man whose virtues he had extolled at every opportunity, ran away to Italy to escape a murder trial.

Pietro took a sip of his beer. Four men at the bar played the Italian game called Fingers: "Cinque!" "Sette!" "Tre!" Each man threw out one, two, or three fingers and at the same time shouted his guess of the total that would show.

Pietro looked at his watch. The library had closed hours ago, of course. He had eight hours to kill before he could get to work.

The bartender brought him another beer. "Pete, you nervous or something?" he asked and gathered up the mess Pietro had made of the first bottle's label.

"I'm sorry, Frank. I didn't know I was doing it."

"Wanta scrape something, go scrape potatoes in the kitchen," the bartender said. "Where you been? Haven't seen you for a long time."

"Studying for exams, Frank," Pietro said and the bartender nodded and went away.

The group playing Fingers had broken up. Only one of the men had stayed, a neighborhood bookmaker who leaned against the wall by the counter reading the *Daily News* and punctuating every other page with a shot of whiskey.

Pietro drank his second beer. He played a game of shuffleboard. He put a quarter in the juke box. He tapped his feet to every measure of every tune that played. He looked at his watch: it was still just a quarter after one.

The bookie turned around and stared at him. Pietro's foot kept tapping. The bookie lit a cigar and called out to Frank. "Turn that goddamned machine off, will you, Frank?"

"He put his money in," Frank said quietly and wiped the bar.

The door opened and one of the girls who sometimes worked the bar came in. Before she even had her coat off, the bookie folded his newspaper and ordered Frank to give her whatever she wanted.

"I'm drinking coffee tonight, Frankie," the girl said to the bartender.

"Whatsa matter, have a tough day, honey?" the bookie called.

She disregarded him.

He pushed off from the wall, and, hanging onto the rim of the bar, edged his way toward the girl. When he reached her, he knocked over the stool at her side as he tried to sit down.

Frankie looked worried. "Easy," he said, "easy."

The girl turned away from the bookie as he righted the stool.

"Don't be a stiff," he said. "Have a drink with me."

He unloaded a handful of bills on the counter before him and pushed forward a ten. "Give 'er a drink, Frankie."

"She doesn't want one, Lou," Frankie said. "She told me she got a headache."

"Who's asking you?" the bookie said to Frank. "You don't want a drink, don't drink," he said to the girl. He put a clumsy hand on her shoulder and she took it away with her fingertips.

"Please just leave me alone," she said evenly.

"Whatsa matter, store closed for the night?"

"I'm telling you leave me alone or I call a cop."

The bookie laughed. "Oh, I like that." He called out to Frank. "She's gonna call a cop, Frankie, what do you think of that?"

Pietro waited.

"I don't want no cops in here, Lou."

The bookie lit a match for his cigar but the flame died out before he could make use of it. "She calls the cops, it's her ass. Not mine."

Frankie gave the bookie another drink, then he mopped the bar in front of the girl. "Honey, why don't you get out of here?" he said.

Pietro got up from his table. "Can I have another beer, Frank?" He put a dollar bill on the counter. "Take out for the coffee, too," he said and waited for the bookie to turn around.

Frankie pushed the dollar away. "Cut it out, Pete."

"I'm paying for her coffee." He looked at the girl.

"Go ahead," she said.

The bookie looked over his shoulder. "Get outa here, kid, before I knock you on your ass."

"You sober enough to try?"

The bookie looked over his shoulder. "Get outa here, to his feet.

Frank started to come around from his side of the bar. "Pete, go home," he said quietly. "Lou, leave him alone, he's drunk."

"I'm not drunk, Frank. Just stay out of this."

The bookie stumbled at him like a truck jumping a curb. Pietro got out of his way as the big arm went back to strike. And then the bookie's face was on him and he slammed at it with both fists, the skull like stone against his knuckles. Blood broke from the nose, and all at once, unexpected, blackness hit the side of Pietro's face, and he was on the floor, and Frank and Jimmy the elevator operator were holding the bookie's flailing arms.

"I'll kill the little bastard, lemme go, I'll kill him."

"That's enough, Lou, he's just a kid, that's enough."

It was gone: the fury that had pushed him into the fight was gone. He watched the blood streaming from the bookie's nose and felt himself sinking into the floor. He couldn't keep his eyes open anymore. "Rocco's dead," he thought, "Mario saw it in the papers."

He woke up in one of the booths, his forehead against the plate glass of the table, a cold wet towel on the back of his neck. His head felt as though it were being rapped with a baseball bat. He opened his eyes. The girl was gone and so was the bookie. Frank was looking at him from the other side of the bar.

"He could have killed you, Pete," he said. "Over that two-bit whore."

When he got out to the street, the early morning air made his head hurt all the more. The neon clock in the window of the Royale was blurred, but he saw the time: six hours remained till the library opened.

He was there alone when the doors were unlocked.

The click of his heels on the Italian marble floor, the vague scent of disinfectant drifting in the high corridors, the murals of the central stairway, the apprehension that fluttered in his chest, the dizziness, the empty stomach and the headache: it all reminded him of the long-ago language of Communion and early Mass.

He took the self-service elevator to the sixth floor and signed the register on the table by the door of the microfilm room. He went directly to the shelves of *The New York Times* Index and found the volume marked 1936. He took it down and helped himself to several call slips from the sleepy librarian's desk, expecting to use them all. Then he sat down and opened the heavy faded-red bound book.

P.

S.

SB.

SBA.

SBACKLEY.

SBAGLIATO, NATALE.

 Suspect in slaying of editor, S 21, 1:2
 Sought for questioning, S 23, 1:3
 Reporter's testimony, S 24, 1:5

Calmly, Pietro copied the notations, seven in all, and closed the index. He stared at the name he had printed neatly on the slips before him, as though afraid of forgetting the object of his research. SBAGLIATO, NATALE: a curious name. He considered it as he would have the title of a poem studied for a written explication. SBAGLIATO, NATALE: mistaken Christmas. Strange that he hadn't seen that before. "Mi chiamo Sbagliato, ma non me sbaglio." *My name is Mistaken, but I am not mistaken.*

A police reporter by the name of Sean O'Neil had witnessed the slaying of Guido Sempione. As the murder car sped away, he had caught a glimpse of a man wearing a yellow flower in his buttonhole. Earlier that same day, the reporter had been in the Centre Street parole office when Natale Sbagliato, a yellow flower in the lapel of his suit, came in for his weekly check-out.

The following day, Sbagliato could not be located for questioning. At his home, police discovered an empty .22 calibre revolver and several notebooks relating to Sbagliato's numbers racket; and on the outside sill of the kitchen window, a flowerbox planted with yellow chrysanthemums.

Pietro shut his eyes. "A coincidence of flowers. But if he didn't do it, why did he run away?" Run away: he was lying in a big bed in darkness. Zia Emilia was saying she would not run away. It was Pappa's bed, empty, deserted. Pappa had run away. Pappa was Natale Sbagliato. The name was before him in history on microfilm. He had killed a man called Guido Sempione. But Pappa was his father, a gentle man, a kiss, a story before bed of a life before his birth. How could he have fired a gun three times point blank at another human being?

Slowly, the objectivity with which he had so carefully covered himself, the detachment with which he had approached the newspaper research, began to melt and in its place slid the terror of Zia Emilia that afternoon of her screams. He was a child again, anxious for his father's return.

He looked out the window of the library room, down onto South Field. Two undergraduates passed a football back and forth, back and forth. They wore sweatshirts and would work up a hot sweat the morning breeze would cool. When they tired, they would go back to the dormitory and take a shower, and then drink a milkshake before going to class. How he envied the lack of complication, the simplicity, the pattern of that life.

He was alone in the microfilm room except for the librarian reading at the table near the door. He thought of Sean O'Neil, the newspaperman who had seen Pappa kill Guido Sempione. Oh Christ, how many men wore flowers in the lapels of their suits those days?

Slowly, his hands without feeling, Pietro put the reels of microfilm back in their brown boxes. He capped his pen and folded away the blank paper he had set before him. He would remember always what he had read. Without the help of notes.

When he got downstairs, outdoors, the college quadrangle was deserted. Classes were in session, the football catch had broken up. He felt cold, his head still ached from the bookmaker's punch. He went to the corner drugstore and ordered a cup of coffee.

It was possible, but improbable, he mused, that the murder of Guido Sempione was unrelated to Pappa's disappearance. Suddenly he slammed down his cup. "Bullshit," he cried to himself. "No more bullshit. No more Zia Emilia. No more Mario. No more bullshit. Too many questions, no answers."

*Sean O'Neil.* How many could there be? He went quickly to the phone book. There was only one and Pietro dialed his number. As he waited through the buzzing at O'Neil's end of the line, he hoped this was the one, the reporter, of fourteen years before. "Maybe he's dead. How old is a reporter?" he asked himself, "forty, forty-five? Then he's fifty-five or sixty now." The phone rang and rang. Pietro finally admitted that Sean O'Neil wouldn't be in at eleven o'clock in the morning. He let the phone

160

ring five more times against the chance he had a wife at home, and then hung up.

He finished his coffee and walked to Riverside Drive. Mothers sat on benches there reading books through horn-rimmed glasses while their children played on the fragile autumn grass. On the river, a tugboat shouldered a string of coal barges north. On the Jersey shore, the Ford sign, ablaze in neon light, ridiculed the sun.

"Wait." Pietro stopped. "Pappa never knew how to drive a car." He turned and ran with all his might back to Broadway, certain of the memory of his father joyfully boasting that someday he would buy a big automobile and Pietro would teach him to operate it. "So how could he have been the driver of the car that goddamn reporter saw?"

He glanced at his watch as he swiftly dialed Sean O'Neil's number again, expecting somehow a miracle that would bring the reporter home for lunch in time to hear his testimony ripped apart by a simple fact; but there was no miracle.

That Pappa never could drive swept over him again and again like a beautiful breeze and kept him fresh and hopeful. Something else to do now: find out if Sempione's murder was ever solved. If it had been, that would be the end of that.

Twenty-seven articles were listed under the name of Guido Sempione for the year 1936. From their titles, Pietro learned Sempione had been a member of the IWW but was never a Communist; that he wrote and printed in his paper massive editorial attacks on the Mussolini regime; that for twenty-five years he had been involved in the organization and execution of every major industrial strike in America; that he had been arrested thirty-nine times;

161

that in fifteen years, seven attempts had been made on his life; that the Communists accused the Fascists, and the Fascists blamed the Communists for the success of that eighth and final try; that his murder remained unsolved.

He read a report of a memorial meeting held in 1946:

### FRIENDS HONOR
### SLAIN EDITOR

Fifty friends and associates of Guido Sempione, anti-Fascist editor, held a meeting in his memory at the Keller School, 9 East 15th Street, and later placed a wreath at 16th Street and Sixth Avenue where he was assassinated ten years ago. His killer has never been brought to justice.

He went out again and began to walk. He walked away from the river. Sean O'Neil lived on Lexington Avenue and about Thirtieth Street judging from the address in the telephone book. At Columbus Avenue, Pietro headed downtown.

It was lunchtime. The sidewalks teemed with children tagging and pushing one another home from school. Pietro recognized the American ones, ragged-hair kids with tight fists ready for their tawny Puerto Rican classmates. Above a store, a window suddenly opened and a mother called down to her child. The boy screamed back in Spanish. It was a familiar scene and reminded Pietro of his own childhood on Grand Street. He stopped and

162

watched the boy detach himself from the group and run to the door of his building, and the window upstairs banged shut. For an instant, he was that boy and he saw Zia Emilia at the embroidery frame in the kitchen, urging him to eat his sandwich, drink his milk.

He shuddered and quickly wiped his hands together as if to awaken himself from the past, from the memory of Emilia fainted. "Please God," he silently implored, "please don't let him have done it," and even as he prayed he knew the hopelessness of his request. If Pappa had killed, nothing could reverse the fact. His eyes felt swollen. There was a heaviness in his throat. He passed the tenement door the boy had run to. A radio was playing upstairs.

He telephoned Sean O'Neil again at one o'clock and again at two. Then, as the end of the day drew near, he dialed the number every half hour.

At six-thirty, his call was answered by the voice of a tired man.

"Is this Sean O'Neil?" His voice trembled.

"Yes. Who's this?"

"*Reporter* Sean O'Neil?"

There was a pause, then, "Who is this?"

"You don't know me. My name is Peter Sbagliato. Could I come . . ."

"Sbagliato?"

"Yes. Could I talk to you for a little while?"

The answer was slow in coming. "If you want to. Do you know where I am?"

"Yes. Would it be all right if I came now?"

"If you want to."

# CHAPTER 8

THE DOORWAY OF SEAN O'NEIL'S BUILDING was sandwiched between a Chinese laundry and a shoemaker's shop. Pietro rang the bell and pushed open the unlocked inside door and was halfway up the first flight of stairs when the buzzer sounded. The hallway smelled of Lysol and cabbage, and under the mat of stained carpeting, the steps creaked.

On the third floor a dark door opened suddenly and silhouetted the tall man against the lamp-lit room behind him. Pietro recognized him at once, from the single meeting years before, though he could not make out his face. This was the one with glowing cigarette always at his lips, who had questioned them in the kitchen about Pappa the morning after Sempione was murdered.

Sean stepped aside as Pietro reached him, and extended his hand. "Come on in," he said quietly.

As they shook hands, Pietro remembered the broad forehead, the deep-set eyes, the shock of graying hair now all white.

"How is your father, do you know?" the big man asked gently.

"We still get letters once in a while," Pietro said. "He's all right."

Sean nodded. "Can I get you a beer?"

"No, thanks."

Sean sat down on the edge of a daybed and pointed out a chair for Pietro. "Fourteen years is a long time," he said. "You were a child."

"I was six." Pietro looked up. Two walls of the room were covered with books from floor to ceiling. A card table by a half-open door to a cupboard kitchen held a typewriter and a coffee cup. "Are you still with the same newspaper?"

"I was canned two months after Sempione was shot. Great business. No, I've been with a trade journal all these years, write a monthly column all my own, a regular Scotty Reston," Sean said quietly. Then he raised his voice. "What did you want to see me about?"

The fact he had been fired gave Pietro sudden confidence. The man smoking before him had lied about the murder car, had been found out and fired. "About my father," Pietro said evenly.

"Ah."

"He didn't kill Guido Sempione."

Sean shut his eyes and leaned his head against the wall behind him. "I never said he did."

"Okay, but you said you saw him drive away from the murder," Pietro insisted.

"No, I never said that either."

"Whatever you said," Pietro shouted, "it couldn't have been my father because he never knew how to drive."

Sean opened his eyes. "You want to know something, Peter?" he asked gently. "The man who killed Sempione that night fired from the seat next to the driver. The car passed me going north on Sixth Avenue and I was on the east side of the street. The killer, the man with the yellow flower, was the man I saw. Not the driver."

"But the newspaper said . . ." Pietro cried.

Sean interrupted him. "Go read it again." He stood up. "Let me get you a beer. I'm going to have one."

"Even so, a yellow flower, that's no proof."

"I agree with you." Sean took two cans of beer from the refrigerator in the closet. "Nobody ever proved anything. The case is still open. Nobody ever even accused your father. He was wanted for questioning and he was never found, that's all."

Pietro took the beer Sean handed him. How easily his father's defense had been dismissed. He had deluded himself with hope and now was once again at the mercy of reality. "But you think he did it, don't you?"

In answer, Sean walked to the window at the end of the narrow room and slowly raised it, and the hussshhh of traffic from Lexington Avenue drifted into the room. "There was never any evidence," he said gently, and turned around. "Look."

Pietro went to the window.

Yellow chrysanthemums grew in a box on the sill. Soot from the city had dusted their faces. He remembered the night of the Festa, when Pappa had gone to the window and picked flowers for both of them.

"The American Legion sells poppies as a reminder of the men who died in the war," Sean said. "I grow these every year as a reminder of a time those men were deceived."

"What do you mean?"

Sean spoke from the daybed again. "Your concern

167

with the murder of Guido Sempione is your father's apparent involvement in it. You don't really know who Sempione was and ordinarily you wouldn't give a damn about his death."

"What are you trying to say?"

Sean held up his hand. "Let's be honest, Peter. People are killed every day. Those who mourn them are those related to them in some way, those who lose something, personally or in a broader sense.

"Do you know who mourned for Sempione?" Sean asked. "The unions mourned him. Why? Because he fought for the rights of working men. Immigrants mourned him because he was their champion. LaGuardia mourned him as a friend and admirer. That's right, Mayor LaGuardia and Sempione were friends. Newspapermen mourned him because he was a fighting editor. The intellectuals and the liberals mourned him because they suspected he was murdered by the Fascists on orders from abroad. And they were right. Edmund Wilson, Dos Passos, Mencken." Sean stood up again and stretched his arms high over his head, and then he went over and shut the window. "When Sempione was killed," he said quietly, "I mourned too. Not so much for him personally, though I was a newspaperman too, as for the moral lapse, for the help we gave his murderers, for the attitude of what's done is done—bury it and forget it."

Pietro set his beer can on the floor. "I don't understand what you're talking about. What's all this got to do with my father?"

Sean smiled. "Not very much. If your father was involved at all, the worst he might have done was kill Sempione. Follow me? We're talking now of political assassination after all, where a murderer is a hero to a certain

168

group of people." Sean paused. "I'm not half as interested in your father as you are," he said. "I'm really not that goddamn interested in whether he killed Sempione or not."

"What about those newspaper stories and your testimony?" Pietro asked angrily. "What you wanted more than anything else was to hang him."

Sean lit another cigarette. "If you're really interested in this thing," he said calmly, "I'll tell you about it."

Pietro leaned back in his chair and gazed across the room at the wall of books that faced him. He felt he was in a college seminar room and Professor O'Neil was about to present and interpret a facet of American history, of international politics, that had never made the textbooks.

"You see, Guido Sempione was marked for murder way back in the early Twenties," Sean began, "from the day he realized Mussolini was taking over Italy. He had his own newspaper even then, a workers' weekly backed by the local chapter of the IWW. He was a natural-born leader of the underdog and he had no trouble turning an awful lot of working class opinion against Mussolini, considering what Benito was doing to the trade unions over there. It didn't take Il Duce long to knock out newspaper opposition in Italy but he couldn't very well close down Sempione's paper in New York."

Sean cleared his throat. "You know, there's an interesting story that goes with an early attempt on Sempione's life," he said. "He was thrown in jail once for libeling a Catholic priest upstate New York. A few days after he was released, he was jumped from behind and got his face slashed with a razor from his left eye down to his collar bone. The man who attacked him was identified by a dozen witnesses in court and yet the man was acquitted. The defense attorney argued God had lashed out at Sempione as punishment for his vicious attack on the Church."

"How the hell did they get away with it?" Pietro asked.

Sean kicked off his shoes and stretched out on the daybed. He shut his eyes. "You've got to understand something," he said quietly, almost to himself. "This was a very fucken patriotic country in the late Teens and Twenties." He shook his head against the dark green covering of the mattress. "We had just won the Great War and were feeling very self-righteous. The hoopla we'd whipped up at years of Liberty Bond rallies didn't disappear overnight. The country was one big national fraternity and the word radical covered the most innocent departure from conformity. You had Russian propaganda, you had the Communist Workers Party."

Sean sighed. "We had a great Attorney-General in those days," he said with heavy sarcasm. "A fellow by the name of Palmer—you may have come across his name in a history book," he said, turning his head to Pietro. "Oh, Attorney-General Palmer was a great American, all right. He was the guy who packed over two hundred and fifty foreigners onto a broken-down steamer and sent them off to Russia. The sentiment he was expressing was the common one of 'if you don't like it here, go back where the hell you came from.'"

He propped himself up on his elbow. "Do you have any idea how many members the Ku Klux Klan had in 1925?" he asked suddenly.

Pietro shook his head.

Sean lay back on the couch. "Over five million," he

whispered. "That's a lot of small minds. I'm talking now of the days of the Scopes Trial, the Scottsboro Case, the mentality that executed Sacco and Vanzetti. But what the hell: they were draft-dodgers, atheists, anarchists. Christ, in those days, any one of those indictments was enough to condemn a man to death.

"Anyway, to get back to Guido Sempione. He spent the years 1914 to 1918 explaining the war to Italian laborers in this country as a squabble over colonial possessions, a capitalists' war, and preaching that the real war for democracy and liberty was being fought by Lenin and Trotsky.

"I'm not defending Sempione," he said as though arguing with himself, almost having forgotten Pietro's presence in the room. "I'm not defending him, I'm not accusing him. I never really understood the sonofabitch. What I'm saying is this country never understood him either and was uncomfortable because he couldn't be pigeon-holed. He was never a member of the Communist Party, he wasn't a paid agitator. He prided himself he never took a dime from a single trade union official. The guy simply was fighting for the rights of labor at a time when God knows the working man needed organizing. It's going to happen someday in this country with the colored people, you watch.

"We tried closing our eyes to him but he wouldn't go away. Mussolini was as unhappy about his existence as we were, though for different reasons."

Sean was quiet for a while and then he smiled sadly and shook his head. "There was only one way to stop him. You had to kill him," Sean said, "and you had to let him be killed.

"That night he was killed, they dragged him in for disturbing the peace at a block party or something. I was

171

hanging around the station house shooting the breeze with the Desk Sergeant. It was almost part of my job. Keep informed. Anyway, they'd worked him over as best they could without being too obvious about it, and they locked him up. I tried to talk to him but he wouldn't have anything to do with me. In a little while the Sergeant got a call ordering him to let Sempione go."

Sean got up and wandered over to the window and looked beyond the yellow flowers on his sill to the traffic on the avenue below. He continued to speak, his back to Pietro. "I've never been sure who that call came from, I mean who originated the release order, the order that allowed the assassination to come off on schedule."

Pietro shut his eyes. "Oh Jesus." Downstairs, the front door slammed. Somewhere in the building a toilet flushed. He heard Sean at the refrigerator getting two more beers. He felt the can of beer cold in his hand and he opened his eyes slowly. "Why were you fired?"

Sean shrugged his shoulders and sat down. "The police got to me first. Unlawful entry: that was for being in your house the day after Sempione was shot. The fact the police had no search warrant was beside the point. Then, interfering with an official investigation, and finally, as far as my paper was concerned, insubordination, refusing to follow orders. Who knows?" He leaned back again on the daybed and made himself comfortable. "I was all piss and vinegar in those days. Fact is, I was never assigned to that case. I followed Sempione that night after he was let go because I felt sorry for him," Sean said, "his glasses broken and himself all beat up. I saw him killed and I reported my hunch—a wild goddamn hunch, granted," he said apologetically to Pietro, "but no one was put on to follow through after we left your house."

172

Sean glanced at Pietro, who remained silent.

"The official investigation was concerned with locating a man called Carlo Materno."

Pietro shook his head slowly. "Who was he?" he asked, not really caring who the man was, sick in his heart for whatever part his father had played in the tragedy of Guido Sempione.

"A Communist agent," Sean said, "a member of their secret police. Evidently, a few days before he was killed, Sempione told a friend he considered Carlo Materno his most dangerous enemy."

Sean crushed out his cigarette. "Carlo Materno was busy plotting the Civil War in Spain at the time of Sempione's murder, but that didn't stop the New York Police from devoting full time to trying to pin the assassination on him, though he was thousands of miles away at the time and they knew it."

Pietro stood up. "You're saying the police purposely went out of their way not to pick my father up and purposely gave him a chance to disappear."

Sean nodded his head.

"But why? Why should they protect him?"

Sean smiled. "I'm afraid you still don't understand," he said. "There was no particular interest in your father himself, one way or the other. A hunt for the real assassin carried with it the dangerous possibility of finding him. This in turn carried with it the danger of exposing the chain of command that had plotted the assassination, a chain of command whose origin was Mussolini himself, in Rome."

"But why were we so afraid to expose the assassination for what it was?" Pietro persisted.

Sean drank from his beer. "What would have been

gained by it, when you come right down to it?" he asked cynically. "There would have been a big stink, a lot of public indignation just at a time when relations between this country and Italy were beginning to run smoothly again. Roosevelt had just lifted the arms embargo that had been imposed during the Ethiopian War. The State Department was about to recognize Italy's claim on Ethiopia.

"Furthermore," Sean concluded, "we were glad to be rid of Guido Sempione. You mustn't forget that; Mussolini had done us a favor. Why rock the boat? Forget it. Let the killer get away. We went after a good Red goat far enough away to guarantee failure."

There was a while of silence, then Sean spoke again. "I know you didn't come here for a history lesson. You were hoping I could tell you something more about your father."

Pietro looked up. "Is there more?"

Sean drew a deep breath as though to brace himself against an unpleasant memory. "The day after I talked to you and your aunt—do you remember that?—the murder car was found on a side street down by the East River. It had been reported stolen two hours before Sempione was killed."

Pietro was startled to hear Sean's sudden laugh.

"You know, I've always loved and admired and respected the Italians," Sean said. "But I still can't figure out why they don't stick to making love and racing sports cars instead of getting involved in things they're just no good at, like war and intrigue. The owner of that car was an undertaker whose place was right around the corner from where you lived."

"Morrone?" Pietro asked, "was that his name?"

174

"Yes, and it was his car." Sean paused and looked at Pietro closely. "Want to know something? That silly ass had a portrait of Mussolini hanging in his back room."

Pietro shrugged his shoulders. "There were a lot of Fascist admirers downtown those days," he said. "It didn't really mean anything. They were proud of new fountains in their village squares in the old country."

"Not that one, Peter," Sean said quietly. "Not because of the portrait, though it was that and the obvious fact he knew your father that prompted me to look around. How that undertaker followed after me in those gloomy rooms, so obviously afraid of what I might find, never even thinking about throwing me out, which is what he should have done since I had no business being there, repeating over and over again like a kid spilling the beans he had gone to bed at ten o'clock the night before—though I never once asked him what he'd done that night."

"Everybody hated him because he used to charge so much for funerals," Pietro said. "They used to say he lived off the dead."

Sean nodded. "I found three thousand dollars in his desk drawer. I found something else, too." He lit a cigarette and slowly waved out the match. "I found a passport."

"What's so unusual about that?" Pietro asked. "Maybe he was going back to Italy."

"It wasn't his passport," Sean said.

"Whose was it?"

Sean paused. "Yours."

"Mine?" Pietro cried. "I never had a passport. How could it have been mine?"

"It was forged. It was never issued by the Govern-

175

ment. I checked on it before turning it in to the police and then I never saw it again. It disappeared and it was never brought up. Officially, it never existed. There is no record of it in police files. When I went back to see the undertaker the next day, he was gone. And that was the day I got the sack."

"But what was he doing with a forged passport in my name?"

"I can only guess," Sean said. "He may have been the contact in New York. The plan may have been for your father and you to live in Italy for a while. Then, because the murder car was seen, they had to get your father out of the country in a hurry. They couldn't risk picking you up." Sean waited. "Does that make sense to you?"

"Yes, it makes sense," Pietro said. "I was supposed to have gone with him. It explains a lot."

"That's my guess," Sean said. "I found out later there had been a double cabin reserved in your father's name on an Italian liner leaving ten days after Sempione was killed. The ship sailed with that cabin empty."

They were silent for a while, Pietro accepting the apparent truth of his father's guilt like a tired swimmer giving himself up to the inevitable sea. Then he slowly rose to his feet. "Thanks for talking to me," he said.

# CHAPTER 9

ON THE GOVERNMENT ROAD TO SALERNO, headlights of speeding cars showed like pairs of dimes in the mountain shadows of dusk.

Giorgio got up from the rock and stepped slowly to the statue of Christ. He struck a match and touched the flame to the wick of the votary candle that squatted in the ruby jar at its feet. "I do this not out of piety," he said as he turned back to Pietro, "but to save some old woman the long walk from the village."

"How so?"

"The flame can be seen from the turn at the start of the hill," Giorgio explained. "During the war they used to come barefoot to light the candle and pray."

Pietro nodded. "Should we be going back?" he asked. "Will he not have come by now?"

"There is still time," Giorgio said. "You will not miss him. After a wait of twenty years, let twenty minutes more pass in peace."

They sat without speaking then, smoking, gazing at the moths that drifted into the circle of light around

Christ's flame. "Your father was a moth," Giorgio murmured.

In a little while he said, "And so the Irishman told you everything that night. Nothing more remained for you to learn."

"When I left him," Pietro said, "I went back to my room and slept until the middle of the next day, I remember."

"And the studies? The lectures?"

"I had no head for college then. I did not know who I was. My face in the mirror was one I recognized as though in memory from a long-ago dream. I had never had a father before, and then suddenly the one I was given was one I could not live with, not even at great distance.

"I went to see Mario like a child running for reassurance to a priest. I told him everything the Irishman had said to me, waiting for a burst of laughter and angry words that would explain away a misconception as he had brushed away my mistaken ideas about my father's involvement with the narcotics."

Pietro swallowed hard. "Instead, two tears fell from his eyes and in a voice choked with misery he confessed there was little more to keep from me. He told me the rest. Of the undertaker, of a man who called himself Tedesco, of Rocco's part.

"When he finished, he went downstairs to the cellar of the restaurant. He returned with a bottle of cognac covered with dust. 'In my country,' he said, 'for courage, they give to men of the infantry three fingers of cognac before an assault. The assault has passed, but better a late drink than none at all. Let me fill your glass now, that you were too young to drink before this.' "

"Bravo Mario," Giorgio said.

"It was good cognac, old and strong, and he poured me another three fingers for my promise never to tell Zia Emilia that I had learned about my father. 'She deceived you fourteen years,' he said to me, 'and now it is your turn to return the kindness.' "

"And you kept your word?"

"Yes," Pietro said. "At this moment, she thinks I am in California. The game goes on, only now it is she who is the child, that good old woman."

Giorgio nodded his head. "Tell me, and the years between that night with the Irishman and today, how did you pass them?"

Pietro shrugged his shoulders. "I have talked so much. Do you really want to know?"

"I have never known you until today except as a photograph," Giorgio said quietly. "I am your uncle, the brother of your father and Emilia. I would like to know, if you feel it in you to speak."

Pietro tried to see the face of his watch.

"There is still time," Giorgio reassured him.

"Okay," Pietro said in English.

Giorgio repeated the expression. "Okay."

"In a way, those were the worst years of all," Pietro began. "How can I explain—my new knowledge deprived me of the birthright of an immaculate father. I could never be President of the United States, do you understand what I am trying to say?"

"Was it shame you felt?"

"No, it was not shame," Pietro said patiently. "I felt as though I had been born at the age of twenty, without parents. I did not know where I was. The studies had no meaning for me, I could not cultivate interest in anything or anyone. I felt nothing to draw from.

"In America, the Korean War had then burst out. I

179

hoped to be drafted. But I saw I would be allowed to finish my studies, because somehow my grades had continued good. So I went voluntarily in the Marine Corps."

"A sin," Giorgio murmured, "a sin to break off the studies."

"Do you know the American Marines?"

"I marinari?"

"No no, they are not sailors," Pietro explained. "These are the shock troops, the corps of infantry that goes in advance, that throw themselves headfirst into fire."

"Ah, like our Bersaglieri, with the plumed beret," Giorgio said. "But why, why the most dangerous division of all?"

"That was the whole idea. A marine is taught to believe with all his heart and soul he is the equal of ten ordinary men. He must believe this in order to survive and function well in battle. In the uniform, in the street, you catch people looking at you with admiration."

Pietro looked up and saw Giorgio with his eyes closed. "The object of the early training was to destroy us as individuals, and then turn us into quick machines that obey commands instantly. It is important that this be so to achieve greatness under fire.

"It was for this process of destruction and rebirth I volunteered. I gave myself up with the ardor of a monk. I tell you I was the best man in my platoon. My rack was tight as the head of a drum and at night I slept on the floor in order to gain time in the morning to polish again the tips of my boots which already caught reflections like a mirror. I was the first to know the number of my rifle and the Articles of War."

Pietro paused. He remembered the recurrent dream.

180

The squad bay was dark, the men around him asleep. He was asleep too, until awakened by the careful opening of the double doors to the passageway. He turned his head. Sergeant Miller was there with the Corporal of the Guard.

"He's not in his rack, Sarge."

"Shhh. The sonofabitch sleeps on the deck. Fix bayonets."

Clack. Click.

"Move out."

Boondocks on the asphalt tile, closer and closer. Suddenly, the flat of a bayonet slapped the sole of his foot.

"Make a sound and you're dead. Get up."

He got up. They marched him to Company Headquarters, naked, in the middle of the night.

In the Captain's office, Sean O'Neil sat behind the desk tapping a brass-tipped swagger stick against the twin bars on his shoulder.

"Prisoner's name, rank, serial number."

"Mistaken, Peter. Private. 1936206."

"Make a note, Sergeant. 'Lying to a commanding officer, appearing before the court out of uniform, improperly addressing an officer.' Anything else you can think of?"

"Yes sir," Miller said. "Resisting arrest, using obscene language, and corrupting the morals of the platoon."

"That's beautiful," the Captain said. "Sbagliato, did you really expect to get away with this? You think changing your name could hide your family history?"

"No sir."

"That's better. Smoke if you have any," the Captain said, and he lit a cigarette.

"I don't have any."

"Tough shit. I suppose you want one of mine."

"No sir."

"Then what're you complaining about? Jesus, you're worse than your father. Tell us about your father, Sbagliato."

"I don't know anything about him, sir."

"Bring in the first witness for the defense," the Captain ordered.

An old woman dressed in black came into the room.

"State your name."

"Emilia Sbagliato."

"Did you know the defendant's father?"

"Si signore."

"Answer in English. Tell the court what you know about him."

"E un assassino chi a deserto suo figlio."

The court laughed.

"Sir," Miller cried. "Being as how's I'm an old Eye-talian myself, I can translate."

The court howled.

"She says she's been in this country forty years and never had no desire to learn the American tongue. She says the defendant's father's an assassinating deserter who worked for Mussolini and Hitler and he pushes dope in Naples on the other side."

"That's a lie," Pietro screamed. "She didn't say anything like that. She said . . ."

"Gag the prisoner," the Captain ordered, and the Corporal of the Guard jammed a bunch of grapes into the prisoner's mouth. "Next witness."

An old man wearing a waiter's apron was led into the room. There was a blue star in the middle of the apron.

"Name?"

"Mario Buonamano."

"I see you have a son in the service."

"Yesa. He's a fight ina war ina Pacifico."

"Thatsa vera nice," the Captain said and the court roared. "Tell us what you know about the defendant's father."

"He'sa bada tomato. He steala t'ree t'ousan dollar. He'sa moonshina. He'sa killa fella man. He'sa run away froma baby boy, leetle bambino."

"You make good spaghetti down at your place, Mario?" the Captain asked.

"Da besta, Capitano. You coma my place, I'ma opena nice a bottle a red wine."

"That's all," the Captain barked and Mario was led out of the court by his apron string, like a dog on a leash.

"If those were the defense witnesses, Sergeant, I don't see any point in hearing the witnesses for the prosecution, do you?" the Captain asked.

Miller saluted. "No sir."

"Slap the prisoner in the brig."

Pietro felt the point of a bayonet cold in the small of his back. He began to march forward. Suddenly the telephone rang on the Captain's desk.

"Captain O'Neil speaking. Good evening, Colonel. Court martialed. I beg your pardon, sir?" The Captain looked up and winked at Sergeant Miller. "Whatever you say, sir. Good night, sir." The Captain slowly replaced the receiver of the telephone, and he began to smile. "You're a free man, Sbagliato," he said gently. "Colonel's orders." He turned to the Sergeant. "Miller, let the impostor go."

"With pleasure, sir."

Now he was alone on the long dark company street. The barracks rose on either side of him like towering tenement walls. Far down at the end of the street, about a half mile away, he could see the main gate and two SP's checking out a vehicle with headlights at half mast. He began to walk toward the gate. The night breeze was cold against his naked skin and he clutched at his dog tags for warmth. They were icy. They were blank and smooth. The ex-prisoner felt for the ball-point pen in his back pocket in order to inscribe his name on the metal plates, but all he felt was the hair on his ass.

He squared his shoulders and began to march: hut do ree fo, hut, hut, hut do. His foot kicked something. He stopped, picked up the butt of a de Nobili and a wooden match. He put the cigar between his teeth and lit it. He took a puff and continued toward the gate, biting off and swallowing tiny pieces of the match in order not to litter the area. Several times he choked as the dry slivers of wood snagged his throat, but he comforted himself with the cigar.

The vehicle that had come through the gate was moving at an unnaturally slow speed, as though the driver was unsure of his destination. Yet it continued to draw closer to the ex-prisoner who soon identified it for what it was—a military hearse. Someone was dead in the squad bay. He bowed his head and stepped respectfully to the side of the street in order to let the hearse slip by.

But it stopped beside him. He watched the driver's window silently slide open and heard a familiar voice whisper, "Come closer to me." He obeyed, took three baby steps forward. Suddenly a silver pistol danced out of the window, froze in front of his head. Before he could move away, a hand formed around its grip, a finger was placed before the trigger, and the gun was fired.

The blinding glare was silent and the ex-prisoner, as

he fell, knew he would be found mysteriously without life in the morning.

And there the dream would end.

Pietro described it quickly to Giorgio who rubbed his arms and murmured, "It chills my flesh."

"It used to chill mine, too," Pietro said. "But it was forgotten the instant I came awake. The day was too filled with action to allow the luxury of self-pity.

"Who knows to what extent the system of destruction and reconstruction was successful with the others," Pietro mused. "Combat is the only honest test. As for me, I knew it had failed me, failed to give me the new life I sought. And I think the reason for the failure was my own enthusiasm that it succeed. In order for the course to be effective, one must resist. One must be killed. Suicide will not do. The chisel of the sculptor bit too easily into soft material and the chips would not fly.

"How I wanted to be taken. I remember full-dress reviews, one in particular. The commanding officer of the base was retiring. The marching band, superb uniforms of scarlet and yellow brilliant in the sunlight, the pennants and the brass, the smell in your nostrils of dust kicked up by cadenced steps, rifle oil and polish, commands called across the open field echoing in such a way only trained ears could understand and pass them along.

"The pageantry reminded me of the Catholic Mass." Pietro paused. "Those who believed were sublimely happy, and saved. I was not moved." He shrugged his shoulders and smiled. "To put it another way, I was like an anxious boy in the arms of a woman—waiting hopelessly for an erection."

185

Giorgio shook his head.

"In spite of everything I was awarded the single chevron of Private First Class, and thanks to my education, the duties of Company Clerk." Pietro cracked the knuckles of his fist. "I spent the war behind a typewriter and rose to the glorious rank of Corporal."

"Someone had to do that work," Giorgio said.

"Calloused fingertips are the battle scars of a woman."

"You would have been happier to have lost an arm or a leg," Giorgio said quietly. "I understand you. In your eyes, your father's debt remains unpaid."

"Three years wasted."

"That you had passed those years in tranquility," Giorgio suddenly cried. He fell to his knees and crossed himself, his eyes open wide to the Christ in candlelight before him. "Ah, my Christ."

Pietro went quickly to his side. "What is it?" he whispered, frightened, "what is it?"

Giorgio spun about and hit him hard in back of the legs and he pitched forward and his hands grabbed dust. "On your knees," Giorgio cried, "on your knees before I strangle you. The score is even, do you hear me? The debt was paid years ago."

# CHAPTER 10

HE HAD WANDERED almost to the next village by the time Annunziata Cafone caught sight of him, stooped in the field, picking the wild chicory he would boil for his evening meal.

"Natale," Annunziata shouted, "Don Natale."

He straightened up slowly, pressing his hand in the small of his back. He took off his hat and used its tattered brim to wing the beads of perspiration from his brow.

Annunziata hurried toward him through the scrub grass. "Damn you," she cried. "Just today you would choose to walk to Naples. Two hours have I spent in search from the moment I thought of finding you." She stopped before him, breathing heavily. "Don Nata," she whispered, "he has come."

The expression on the old man's face did not change.

"Pietro, your son from America. He is here, in Masinalto," Annunziata said, "do you understand me?"

Slowly, he nodded his head.

"And with what a car." Annunziata slapped her face in admiration. "A new machine, the color of fire, with an open top that lets in the sun. And how he speaks Italian. Like one of us," she cried. "Hurry, hurry to Christ by the road, where he waits for you with Giorgio." Annunziata reached out for the old man's hand, but he drew it away. Then she saw the tears in his eyes. "Very well," she said, "come alone. But come quickly. I must go back to cook for my men."

Natale Sbagliato watched her scuffle away and then disappear over the ridge by the road, her feet kicking up a low, lingering cloud of dust. He leaned over and picked up his harvest bag, a gunny sack quarter-filled with the withering yellow-green chicory weeds, staple food of the very poor. Slowly, he began to follow Annunziata's path.

Thank God he has finally come, Natale murmured to himself. His gratitude was like that of a condemned man embracing his day of execution. The waiting was over: now only the final punishment remained. He had never doubted that one day Pietro would come across the sea to the village of Masinalto and find him there, without words to ask forgiveness, a piece of man decayed. Now he had come, and he, Natale the father, was to meet him by the statue of Christ by the hillside.

Step by step, his thoughts wandered back to another statue, one trailing dollar bills. The memory of that Festa night was fresh in his mind, tended as it had been through the years with suffering, like flowers growing on a grave. It was a memory redolent with the expectation of glory, of red lights and green, of a six-year-old boy in the lap of his aunt, of terror, of a trigger giving way to the pull of a finger, and the bearded face of a man with eyes half-shut for a better look at the one who had called his name, exploding in a flash of fire.

188

"Faster, faster," he had screamed, still gripping the wrist of his own gloved hand that had taken Sempione's life like the wrist of an enemy that threatened his own life, *"Gesu Cristo mio,* that we have been seen."

"Shut up, damn you. Do you want me to kill us both? I'm going as fast as I can," the American driver of the car shouted back. "Throw that goddamn gun out the window soon's I turn the corner. And shut up."

The car nearly turned over as it screeched around the corner, and Natale had to be told again to throw the gun away. Once his hand was free of it, his terror began to quiet and he took deep breaths, like a man rescued from the sea. He found himself listening intently to the sounds of the night, expecting to pick out of the darkness the faraway wail of a police siren. The car turned another corner and the driver slowed down to normal speed. "We're all right," he said.

"Where do we go now?"

"I suppose you want me to drive you home," the driver said. "We stay together till we ditch the car and then you go anyplace you want. Just don't come with me, I don't know you. Understand?"

Natale nodded his head. They were in traffic now. They slowed down and stopped for a red light. There was a policeman on the corner. Natale shut his eyes tight and words of prayer unrecited since childhood formed silently on his lips as he begged escape. The car began to move. They were safe.

In a while, the driver turned onto a side street and parked by the river's edge. He turned off the ignition but left the keys in the lock. "Now we get out of the car and go together to the corner," he said. "Then I go that way"—he pointed north—"and you go that way. Understand?"

Natale said he understood. It was not until he was out of the car and walking that he realized his body trembled, that his knees rolled under his weight.

Now the driver was gone. Natale did not turn to see him go. He found Grand Street and began the walk downtown, passing stores and buildings he had passed before on walks, blind to them now, conscious only of the long street before him.

Near Mulberry Street, the neon face of a clock in a jeweler's window began to wake him up. Less than an hour had gone by since he had left the sound of trumpets and joy, the laughter and singing of the Festa de San Gennaro. Now he was back and the music was still. It was as if the Festa had never been, the streets dark and empty. Only the arcs that curved across the sky, like the metal work of a wedding band bereft of diamonds, bore testimony to a celebration past. And now, though he had done what he had been made to do in that time, he was still Tedesco's prisoner.

He found Morrone's entrance and stepped into the undertaker's parlor. He crossed directly to the light-rimmed door he had passed through earlier and without knocking went into that back room.

Tedesco and Morrone were playing cards at the big table. Three glasses and an unopened bottle of champagne were at the undertaker's elbow.

Tedesco saw Natale in the doorway and he slowly set his cards on the table. "E beh?" he whispered, "so?"

Natale did not move, and he did not speak. He watched Tedesco's mouth twitching impatiently, and when he pushed away his chair, jumped to his feet and

190

shouted "Answer me." The collector stepped forward and murmured, "It is done," sorry to end the other's suspense.

Tedesco was jubilant. "Bravo," he cried. He hurried to Natale's side. He pumped the collector's hand and pounded his back with joy. "Bravo, Don Natale. Tonight you have served your country in a manner few men before you ever have." He turned to the undertaker. "Open that bottle of champagne, quickly, for we celebrate the death of an enemy and the birth of a hero." He drew Natale into the room and shut the door behind them.

Morrone picked up the bottle and began work on its cork. He nodded at Natale and murmured, "Congratolazione."

Tedesco slapped his hands together. "Ah, that Rocco was right. He said you would not refuse and you did not. How well he knew his man."

Natale lowered himself into a chair. "I was given no choice. I had no heart for tonight's work," he said.

"Ah, but now." The words exploded from Tedesco with a great laugh. "Now how do you feel?"

Natale shook his head. "I feel nothing. Only self-disgust, and fear."

Tedesco picked up a glass of champagne and with a wave of his free hand dismissed Natale's words. "You have killed a hornet. Had you lacked the courage to do so, self-disgust would have been appropriate. As for your fear," Tedesco said, handing Natale the glass of bubbling wine, "you have nothing to fear. Listen to me. Your sweet son sleeps safe in his own bed, thanks to you. Now the rest is for us."

Without waiting for the toast he knew Tedesco would propose, Natale raised his glass and drank it off like water. Then he wiped his mouth with the back of his hand, leaned forward, and set the empty glass back on the table. "I am happy the rest is for you," he said quietly as Tedesco refilled his glass, "for we were seen."

Tedesco looked up quickly and put the bottle down. "You were seen? What do you mean, you were seen?" he stammered.

Natale nodded his head. "Just so. Seen. Do you know what the word means? As Sempione fell dead, a person saw us as we drove away," he said.

"And you wait till now to tell me?" Tedesco shouted.

"The champagne would not have been opened otherwise."

"Imbecile."

Morrone ran to the door and locked it. "What are we going to do?"

"And that you lock the door, idiot, what do you think you accomplish?" Tedesco buttoned his collar and drew up his necktie. "Can it be locked from the other side?" he asked as he put on his coat.

The undertaker nodded his head and reached into a pocket for his key ring. He began to separate that key from the rest. Tedesco grabbed them all from his hands. "What use do you think you'll make of any of them in my absence?" he demanded. Morrone showed him the key that fit that lock and Tedesco ordered him to keep Natale away from the telephone.

"There is no one I could call," the collector murmured.

Tedesco hurried out of the room, and as they heard the lock turning on them, Natale picked up the glass Tedesco had filled for him and emptied it as he had emptied the first. "Do you know," he said quietly to the undertaker, "I feel a calm I have never felt before."

192

"But are you losing your mind?" Morrone demanded. "Do you know we could all go to the electric chair?"

Natale nodded his head. "That is what I mean," he said. "My future is secure. I know the best and the worst that can happen to me. And I have no control over what is to come."

"And in your mind, what is the best that can happen now?" the undertaker asked. "A parade in your honor along la Via dei Imperiali? A reception by Il Duce"—he glanced at the portrait of Mussolini hanging over the sideboard—"in il Palazzo Quirinale? Fame? Riches? A villa in Como?"

Natale closed his eyes and shook his head slowly from side to side. "My dear Morrone, no," he said quietly. "To return to my son and to my sister and the life that was mine two days ago. Only now without the yearnings for greatness and distinction you enumerate, yearnings that used to poison happy days."

Morrone laughed. "That you forget that life. Better to think of adapting yourself to the glory of Rome."

"What do you mean?" Natale shouted.

The undertaker slammed his hand against the table and stood up. "Did you think, honestly, that you would be permitted to return to the streets collecting penny bets and chatting with knowing tongue with the local peasants? Did you imagine Tedesco would risk your talk in the days to come, that Rocco Gargatto, knowing you as he does, would allow you to remain in this country with your secret knowledge and guilt-ridden heart capable of bringing about the greatest scandal since the death of Matteotti?" The undertaker poured himself a glass of champagne. "You saw your passport with your own eyes."

"But the passport was in the event something went wrong."

The undertaker smiled.

"I myself was not seen," Natale shouted. "The darkness. I, I covered my face with my arms, I swear to you. The car was seen, that is all."

"Your words are wasted on my ears, Collector. We must wait for Tedesco."

"But what am I to do, what am I to do?"

"Concentrate on that great calm you spoke of minutes ago, and the fact that truly you have no control over what is to come." The undertaker raked together the cards that lay scattered on the table, and he shuffled them. "A hand of Brisk? We must pass the time until the Colonel returns."

"My family. When do I see them?"

The undertaker shrugged his shoulders. "Who knows?" he said. "Who knows?"

Natale glanced at the telephone behind Morrone. "Do me this favor," he said. "Call Mario—you know him, Mario Buonamano who has the cafe. Ask him to tell my sister not to worry, that I am well."

Morrone raised his eyes from the hand of Solitaire he had dealt himself. "What did Tedesco say?"

"But *I* will speak to no one. *You* speak to Mario."

The undertaker's eyes returned to his cards. "The telephone will not be used."

"Look, it is almost three o'clock in the morning," Natale pleaded. "Emilia will be worried. Just say I will be home very late."

"You are a master of understatement," Morrone murmured. "Certainly this is not the first time you have stayed away all night."

"No, but who knows what she is thinking."

194

"There is no reason for her to think other than she has thought on the occasion of your other absences," Morrone said impatiently. "She will receive word of you when the time comes. I repeat, the telephone will not be used."

The collector leaned his head against the back of his chair and covered his face with his hands. Against his fingers, he could feel the throbbing pulse of his eyes. He heard the undertaker's cards being snapped one by one on the table. From the corridor outside the chapel came three notes of the chiming clock. "What have I done?" his mind moaned, "what have I done? That I find myself closed up this way with a man my stomach cannot take, locked away from Pietro my only son, threatened with a life I killed a man in order to bring about and now no longer want." Suddenly it seemed a darkened chamber in his mind went wild with light, revealing like a loop of film run over and over again, Sempione's blasted face reeling back from the gun in his, Natale's, hand. This he had done, this he had done; and he recognized that irrevocable act as a step over the edge of a precipice. He felt himself falling.

He took his hands away from his eyes and saw the undertaker playing the cards. Time passed. The chiming clock of the chapel sounded four times. The champagne, its chill gone, had long ago been finished.

Then they heard the street door open and shut. Morrone went quickly to the door and braced his shoulder against it, gripped the knob tightly with both hands as the key was turned in the lock on the other side.

"Damn you." They heard Tedesco swear and Morrone let the door swing open. "What devil did you expect I was?" Tedesco demanded angrily.

"Excuse me," Morrone murmured.

195

Tedesco stepped into the room, his eyes fastened on the collector. "Your great horticultural love had escaped me completely," he said gently and nodded as Natale glanced down at the chrysanthemum in the lapel of his jacket. Suddenly his hand sprang out and snatched away the yellow flower and his fingers mashed the petals into shreds before Natale's face. "They are looking for you," he screamed, "for you and your vanity. Tremble, piss in your pants with fear, that God damn the day Rocco learned your name."

"But how do you know it is this one they look for?" Morrone cried. "Do they know where he is?"

Tedesco spun about and slammed his open hand across the undertaker's face. "Who is it that asks questions here?" he shouted. "Now listen to me, both of you. You do exactly as I say or I see to it personally that you are cut into a thousand pieces.

"You, Undertaker, you have a vacant coffin here?"

Morrone nodded his head. "In the cellar."

"And some heavy wood, a hammer, nails? A drill, an auger?"

"There should be."

"Now listen to me. Go below. Fit small blocks of wood to the bottom corners of a casket so it will sit raised from the floor an inch or two. Then with the drill make several holes the size of your finger along the underside of the box, to permit the entrance of air. Now go."

"My keys to the cellar," Morrone murmured, and Tedesco handed them over.

"No," Natale screamed, "no, ah no."

Tedesco turned to him. "Then you understand the plan, Collector? Now hear these words. If it were to me, I would have you carted out without air. It is your dear and loving friend who planned my expedition here that saves your life. Rocco's orders to me were to see you escape unharmed. I am doing my best."

Tedesco looked closely at his watch. "In exactly one hour and twelve minutes, three of our friends from the Consulate will arrive to help. We must be ready for them."

Through the open cellar door came the rasping sound of wood being sawed. Tedesco smiled. "It must tear at his miserly heart to destroy one of his precious coffins. But look how pale you are, my dear Collector. Set your mind at ease, I beg of you. Here, a glass of champagne. Ah, the pig below has drained the bottle."

In a while, the sawing stopped and Morrone called, "Colonel, I need your help."

Tedesco took Natale's arm, led him to the cellar steps, and followed him downstairs.

A single bare bulb hung from the ceiling and showed Morrone, his sleeves rolled back to his elbow, a saw in his hand, standing above a coffin swathed in a thick quilted pad. "It weighs too much for one to turn it on its side."

Tedesco pulled away the padding and touched with admiration the deep cross carved in relief on the heavy lid. "Transportation fit for the Pope," he said. "Look, Sbagliato, the respect the undertaker pays you."

"The others are made of metal and would not take the drill," Morrone muttered. "This piece cost me five hundred dollars."

"Send us a bill in Rome," Tedesco said. He turned to Natale. "Come, Collector, lend a trembling hand. Ah, but first you must open your eyes, eh? Feel, just feel the quality of this fine purple satin. What pasha's limousine has upholstery like this?"

Under Tedesco's supervision, the coffin was tipped

over and fitted with its blocks of wood, and the holes for air were drilled in its floor. Morrone insisted the casket be wrapped again with its quilt to protect it against scrapes as they carried it upstairs, and Tedesco laughed at him. "Kiss it goodbye, friend," he said, "this is one you will never sell."

Natale turned away and slowly climbed the stairs, ignoring Tedesco's angry order that he help them carry the coffin. Dazed, he listened to their complaining oaths as they strained under the weight of the big box. He prayed it would not fit through the cellar door.

It did. They set it down on the floor at his feet. He watched Tedesco and the undertaker dry their faces of perspiration. Tedesco told Morrone to bring out another bottle of strega, that they needed a drink. He promised Natale that Rocco would hear of his refusal to help carry the casket upstairs.

Morrone filled the glasses. Tedesco put one in front of Natale. "Wet your throat with this. Instantly."

Natale swallowed the sweet burning liqueur.

Tedesco took a small envelope from his pocket and emptied it on the table. Two capsules tumbled out. He pushed them toward Natale. "Take them with another drink," he ordered.

"What are they?"

"Poison," Tedesco shouted. "Swallow them before I push them through your eyes."

Natale put the capsules on his dry tongue. They felt like two bits of wood. He poured strega into his mouth and swallowed the capsules.

"They will ease your nerves and make you sleep," Tedesco said. "Believe me, the worst has passed." He tapped the coffin gently with his foot. "You will think of it as a warm and comfortable bed. And in a few hours, like Lazarus, you will rise from the dead." He picked the collector's crushed chrysanthemum up from the floor and dropped it into the casket. "Pity your taste does not run to white carnations." He examined his wristwatch. "We have made good time. Our friends will be here shortly and we are ready for them."

He turned to the undertaker and ordered another strega. He held the glass to Natale's mouth and carefully tipped it forward. "That it quickens the work of our miraculous pills," he said. "How are you, Collector?"

Natale felt a smile with the taste of strega creep across his lips. "But Pietro?" he asked.

Tedesco took a single cigarette from his shirt pocket and placed it between the collector's lips. "You will see him soon," he promised quietly.

"Colonel," Morrone whispered, "he smokes only cigars."

Tedesco lit Natale's cigarette. "This is better than the best toscano. Draw on it deeply, Collector, that it does you good."

He inhaled the sweet warm smoke, once, twice, and he saw a sunset in his mind. The day was done and he was safe. Pietro too. The memory of Sempione killed came to him as a delicate thrill. Rocco was pleased. Natale Sbagliato was a savior. How simple it had been to redeem the years of greenhorn humiliation.

Tedesco, himself a great Italian, was helping him to his feet. A final puff of smoke, if you please. Thank you. Si si si, one must step carefully into the limousine. Just so. Now to be seated and prepare oneself for the parade of gratitude. Rest the head for ultimate comfort. Ahhhh. And now the arms arranged across the chest in the salute of a Grand Marshal. Marvelous. Close the door for privacy. A magnificent sight! Swords and shining helmets,

199

the muffled tones of marching feet close at hand, mighty stallions lifting spirits to the sky. This is the Italy we have made with honor. What movement, how it carries one along. A jolt now and then, but nothing. Rest assured. The cobbled streets. . . . What can one expect? Excellent! A review of the Imperial Fleet. Si si si, the blasts of the vessels' horns are clear. We sail the seas in splendor now, unlike the cattleboats that carried away the simple peasants of another age. My dear Rocco, I am honored. *Honored.*

The gunny sack Natale carried slapped at his knee with every step. He fixed his eyes on the shattered tips of his shoes as he walked, as he thought of those few days of joy after his awakening.

At first he had experienced an overwhelming fear that he had been buried alive, that water had seeped into his grave. Indeed, warm water lapped gently at his naked body. The darkness was because his eyes were closed. Ah, what pain to open them, a hundred hammers pounding at his brain.

"Signor Commendatore." A girl's voice. "How do you feel now?"

The face of an angel was close to his.

"A most extraordinary bon voyage party, eh?" The girl laughed. "Do you feel strong enough to stand now? Come, I will help you up. I pray I find you in better form tonight. Am I understood?" she asked with a smile.

He felt her strong hands under his arms and he raised himself out of the bathtub. The girl began to rub him swiftly with a thick white towel big as a blanket. When she had dried him to her satisfaction, she helped him into a dressing gown of scarlet silk and directed his

200

feet into leather slippers lined with fleece. Then she took his hand and led him out of the bathroom into an adjoining double bedroom bright with sunlight that streamed in through a bank of circular windows above a wall-long couch.

"Where are we?" Natale heard himself ask.

The girl smiled and caressed his face. "A day and a half out of New York and less than seven away from Genova. What more do you want to know? My name is Anna. The barber will be here in five minutes. Please," she said, "let him only shave you and not touch your hair, that I like it long." She handed him a glass of water and a small pink tablet. "With the compliments of Colonel Tedesco."

Natale sighed and swallowed the tablet.

"Do you wish me to help you dress?"

Natale shook his head and shut his eyes. When he opened them, Anna was gone.

He found a note pinned to the coverlet of the enormous bed. "How do you like the service of our Italian ships? With luck, the clothes in your closet fit as they should. They, like Anna, are yours. We meet again at dinner. *Viva!*"

That night, an orchestra played in the grand salon and violins serenaded the Captain's table in the center of which was a monumental arrangement of yellow chrysanthemums. "In your honor, Commendatore," the Captain said with a bow, and Tedesco covered his smile with his hand. "That they please you, and that you have a comfortable crossing. We are honored by your presence on board."

Wine was poured. Tedesco proposed a toast to the illustrious Commendatore Sbagliato. "One day soon you will learn of his heroic act, of the manner in which this modest man responded to the call of his Motherland. For now, let us drink to his patriotism and the inheritance of glory this Italian father passes on to his descendants."

Tears filled Natale's eyes. The dream that had become a nightmare was dream again come true. Tedesco leaned across the table. "Who knows what bitter lemon Morrone sucks this very instant," he whispered, and then he laughed and Natale laughed too and squeezed Anna's hand which under cover of the table cloth had climbed high inside his thigh.

Dinner was of seven courses, with as many wines served by silent stewards wearing navy coats of velveteen. There was dancing and much laughter, and a table of roulette at which Natale was permitted to win five hundred lire—more money than he'd had in his pocket since the days before the Wall Street crash.


The sound of an automobile slowing as it approached him caused Natale to raise his eyes from the road. Beyond it, silhouetted against the sky, was the statue of Christ, his destination. The car was an American convertible, its top lowered, and it rolled almost to a stop as it edged closer to the side where he walked. A woman with a kerchief tied around her head against the wind sat beside the driver, her husband. "They will ask directions," Natale said to himself, "and I with no tongue for an answer." Suddenly the woman raised a camera to her face and Natale heard the click of his picture snapped. Then the woman smiled and mispronounced the word for thanks. "He's so ragged, honey, give him something." The husband shrugged his shoulders. "I don't have any

202

change," he said, and the car whipped away into the road and was gone.

Natale sighed and fixed his eyes on the dark Christ where Pietro waited. He pushed his mind to thoughts of Rocco.

His old friend had not changed at all in the three years they had been apart. They had embraced, kissed one another's cheeks in heartfelt joy of reunion. "Like old times," Rocco had cried in English and slapped Natale's back, squeezed his hand, straightened his necktie of hand-painted silk.

"Let me look at you, Nat. Ah, that's better." He unbuttoned Natale's coat and held it open, smiled happily at the sight of the monogram NS embroidered on the pocket of the cream shirt. "They got 'em done in time. That's good. Nat, that penny-ante downtown lottery shit was not for you." Rocco laughed. "I'da had your brains blown out if you didn't do this job."

"I would not have let you down, Rocco," Natale said, "after all you did for me."

"Go on, you had to be pushed head first," Rocco said with a laugh. "But I knew it would be so." He spoke Italian now. "I understand you, Natale, your wish to lift yourself, to do something for the Old Country, to make things easier for the boy." He picked a cigar from the humidor on his desk and bit off its tip. "But I knew too, inside, the softness of your heart.

"About the boy. Believe me when I say I am sorry he is not with us now. But listen to what I say. Take a vacation for a while. Travel around. Enjoy yourself. In weeks, a matter of a month or two, whenever you say, we send for him. Your sister too, if you insist." Rocco wrinkled his nose. "I remember her as a pain in the ass. She and Anna would not see eye to eye. Ah, Anna. Do you like her, does she please you?"

Natale smiled. "I have never known a woman like that one."

"Well, think of her as you would a pair of shoes. If she begins to pinch, or if you tire of her style, or of her color for that matter," Rocco laughed, "let me know. I will send you to the shoemaker and you can try on what you like.

"To return to the subject of your son. He is taken care of. I have established a trust fund in his name at the Bowery Bank in New York, just like the Americans," Rocco said with a smile. "There will always be money for his college, eh? Meanwhile, send them in cash whatever you want. We live like millionaires here, as you can see." He stood up and pointed at the ancient chest of drawers across the room. "From the monastery at Monte Cassino," he said, and then raised his finger to the painting of Benito Mussolini that hung above it. "From an impoverished village in the North. Ooopila! A sacrilege! Take it less seriously, friend of mine, that you enjoy life more. You should see him these last few days, ecstatic over the false victories of his Black Arrow division in Spain. The German's tanks blast their way through Republican lines and *that* one pushes in behind them the reluctant infantry of the Italian Army. When the world is not laughing at us, Natale mine, it sees us with contempt. Ah, I shock you. I am a realist—economically, politically, morally, and militarily—and you and Il Duce are idealists. Good luck to both of you."

In a few short months, satisfaction from the opulence of his new life began to fade and Natale felt again the unrequitable longing that had marked him for service for Rocco Gargatto. His mission had been accomplished and now he was like a starving man before whom a banquet is spread, who rises, in spite of himself, hungry from the table.

He suffered with the memory of Guido Sempione. And although his heart was bursting with desire to see Pietro, the decadence of that atmosphere was unhealthy for a child. And how explain the good fortune? Natale vowed to himself the boy would never know his father had killed in cold blood.

One Saturday afternoon in early spring, he felt a sudden desire to close himself in the darkness of a confession booth and speak aloud to a priest of the Church the sins that blackened his soul. At the foot of a narrow street, he found a church, ancient and small, and passed through its narrow door into the cool, stone-walled interior, dipped his fingers in the basin of holy water, made the Sign of the Cross. He took his place behind three children and waited his turn at the single confessional. Across the aisle, an old woman wrapped in a black wool shawl prayed for peace and the return of her son from Spain.

The children passed through their confessions one by one, and returned grinning from the altar rail and their quick penance, hurrying to resume their play outdoors. Natale rose slowly from his knees and parted the curtain into the booth and knelt before the profile of his confessor. He bowed his head and blessed himself in a whisper, and then drew a deep breath.

"Padre, this is my first confession in many years."

The priest nodded his head and without raising his eyes, glanced at the expensive fabric of Natale's suit.

"I do not know where to begin."

"With your most grievous sins," the priest murmured, "and the specific one that prompted this confession. Do not be afraid, my son."

Natale shuddered. The palms of his hands clasped before him were damp with perspiration. "I, I have stolen money."

"Much money?"

"Yes, Father."

"Has it been returned?"

"No, Father. It happened long ago. In America."

"Go on."

"I have committed adultery."

"How many times?"

"I do not know, Padre. Many times."

"Does your poor woman know?"

"She is dead, Father."

"Ah."

"I have missed Mass, eaten meat on Fridays . . ."

"Yes . . . yes . . . yes . . ."

"I have lied to my only son, Father."

"Yes . . . yes . . . go on."

Natale shut his eyes and the closeness of the confessional moved in on him like the dark walls of a coffin. He heard the breathing of the priest; it seemed to come from another world.

"I am waiting for you, my son," the priest murmured.

"I have taken another's life."

The priest turned his head toward Natale but averted his eyes. "How do you mean, you have taken another's life?" he asked hesitantly.

Natale paused and then found the courage to speak plainly. "I have committed a homicide."

The priest crossed himself. "You must understand that your confession to me is not enough," he said. "I cannot grant you absolution until you have confessed before the civil authorities as well."

Natale raised his head and saw the face of a young man: the priest was little more than a boy. "The civil authorities of what country?"

"Lower your voice," the priest said. "You are at confession in the house of God."

"But is that confession not enough to ease the suffering of a tortured man?"

"I tell you you must admit your guilt to the police."

"And I tell you my sin was sanctioned, excuse me, *commissioned*, by the Imperial Fascist Government of Italy."

The priest's hands shot up to his ears, and he shut his eyes. "Enough," he hissed, "enough."

"What is it?" Natale cried. His hands broke from their attitude of prayer and he clenched them into fists. "You deal with the simple sins of children—masses missed, forbidden thoughts of the flesh. But you find my problem is too grave. Shall I take it to a cardinal, a bishop? Will they find it in their power to lift me to a state of grace?" Natale's trembling voice broke into a sob. "Or am I to be eternally lost?"

The priest reached out and touched Natale's arm. "Please," he whispered urgently, "please, you must control yourself. In these times," he said, "these times of war..."

"Which war?" Natale moaned.

The priest turned his head away. "Forgive me," he said, "I cannot grant you absolution. Pray for me, as I will pray for you."

Natale got up from his knees. "That you be damned," he whispered.

The priest, for protection, again made the Sign of the Cross.


Overnight, it seemed, the German tourists who had crowded the cafes with their guttural Italian suddenly appeared in uniform, the mark of the swastika banded round their arms, their boots tapping insolently against Italian pavement, their cameras replaced by silver-handled daggers and revolvers in polished leather. They took the best wine, the best women, the best seats at the Opera. Less than eleven months after Mussolini's entry into the war, the Italian Empire was irrevocably demolished.

On the day the Government was reorganized to German specifications and shifted north to Milan, Natale began his long slow walk back to the village of his birth. His journey was interrupted in Naples by the full-page news-photo of Il Duce dangling by his ankles from the girder of an unfinished gasoline station.

In Masinalto, the poverty of peacetime was remembered as a time of plenty. Before the arrival of American troops, stray dogs had been slaughtered and roasted, the children led to believe the meat they ate was billygoat. Now there was an abundance of chocolate and chewing gum and powdered eggs.

"But how do you find yourself in our midst?" Giorgio cried as he embraced Natale his brother, "that I thought you lived in luxury on the other side?"

"Ah, brother mine," Natale whispered, "what a long unhappy story my explanation makes. I will confess it to you when the courage comes to me."

The day of his arrival, Giorgio accompanied him to the local office of the Allied Military Government, set up in the Mayor's house, to register his presence in Masinalto. The young American lieutenant there spoke Italian learned in college, and spoke it poorly. Natale answered his first question in English, and then explained he had lived in America many years, and that he had just come down that day from Rome where he had worked as bookkeeper in a building which had been destroyed by bombs.

The lieutenant took him by the arm and led him into the office of the captain, and five minutes later, Natale was employed by the United States Army as an interpreter, with salary to be paid in food rations.

Those first days, it seemed to Natale he had never been away. The long-ago misery of stifled ambition had simply been replaced by disillusionment and the suffocating memory of Guido Sempione, and an impossible longing for a deserted son. But this his present grief was magnified by tears of realization that a mistake had been made, his life now almost gone. His eyes shut with shame, he explained to Giorgio the truth of his presence in Italy.

And then one morning, just before dawn, he was awakened by the sound of a jeep racing to a stop outside his window. He listened as the crunch of boots in the stony path approached his door, and he knew he had been discovered. He froze with fear. They would send him back to America to stand trial for the murder. Pietro, fifteen years old, would see in the newspapers the picture of his father behind prison bars. Natale gripped his ragged jacket about him in a half-conscious attempt to disappear. His eyes searched the four corners of the room for escape, for death. There was nothing. The knock on the door fell like a rock on a coffin. He rose up. A plan scrambled through his head: once outside, he would break into a run and the Military Police would shoot him dead. There would be no picture. Anxiously, he went to the door and lifted the bar from across the jamb.

He was hit instantly in the stomach by the point of a submachine gun. Behind the gun was an Italian, his face unshaved. He was backed by two others gripping guns at the ready. Slips of red ribbon were tied in the button-holes of the discarded Army jackets they wore against the morning frost.

"Natale Sbagliato?"

His head ducked involuntarily. "Si."

The one with the submachine gun stepped aside in the doorway. "Outside, quickly," he said, "move it."

"Let him put on his shoes."

"What difference will it make?" said the one with the big gun.

"Put on your shoes."

Natale obeyed this last command, but his trembling fingers were unable to tie the laces. He straightened up as the gun pressed in his back urged him to move outside.

In the half light of dawn, Natale saw the markings of the American jeep were painted over. Communist partisans. There was no need to run; death at their hands was guaranteed.

He was seated up front, next to the driver, and the jeep spun about in the tight road and headed north. "Where do you take me?" Natale asked, and he was given no answer. He knew from their accent they came from close to Naples. His only wish now was that they would kill him quickly, close to Masinalto, so Giorgio would learn of his death, instead of taking him to Naples first.

Just beyond the village, the jeep slowed down as it passed an American patrol, and the partisans and the soldiers called out to one another. Then they picked up speed again. A few kilometers went by in silence, and then one of the men in back said, "There, on the right," and the jeep turned off the road onto a cleared path that cut through the brush and stunted trees of the hillside. They drove on for a quarter of an hour, the one in back with the submachine gun cursing the bucking of the jeep as it climbed the twisting pot-holed path. Then they stopped.

Natale was led around to the far side of the mountainous outcropping of rock they had parked beside. There was a clearing there, room enough for five men to stand in a wide circle. The fifth man, the leader, stood by a wood fire, drinking steaming coffee from a battered cup. "A happy return to the province of your birth," he said. "Not much changed these thirty years, has it? That putrefying side of animal never made it to the South. His only look here was upside down." He took a step forward and stared hard at Natale. Then he turned to the man with the submachine gun. "Are you sure this is the one?"

"His name is Sbagliato."

"Why is he not pissing in his pants?" the leader said. He looked back at Natale. "You killed Sempione?"

One of the others muttered, "What do you expect him to say?"

Natale thought of the young priest in Rome. He nodded his head.

The leader finished his coffee and lit a cigarette. "What do you do now?"

"I work as interpreter for the Americans."

"Do they know who you are?"

"By name only."

211

One of the men spit into the fire. "What do we wait for?" he demanded of the leader, and released the safety of the automatic pistol slung around his neck.

"To end his life is a kindness," the leader answered, and put his hand before the barrel of the man's weapon. "And the Americans find him useful. Let him continue his work for them, only now with the *written* word." He put his cigarette between his teeth and unsheathed the bayonet at his belt. "Take him by the arms," he ordered.

Natale backed away. "Kill me," he screamed, "kill me as I killed Sempione." He kicked out as his arms were pinned behind him, and then one of the men fought his feet and gripped his legs together.

"Hold his head."

A vise closed around his throat, fingers knotted in his hair. He could not move. He watched with horror as the bayonet came in toward his face, saw the bright edge honed along the rust-pocked blade. Suddenly the leader's free hand lashed out and squeezed the flesh of his face hard between his teeth. The hand tightened on his throat and bitter bile spilled from his tongue. The bayonet hesitated. Then struck.

He felt an instant of ice, and then the warm blood spurting. The men who held him let him fall and he rolled on the wet red earth, screaming for death.

"It makes more sense than a burst of lead."

"Let us go now for the Americans or they find him like an empty bottle, the way the blood pours."

The engine of the jeep barked in the stillness.


Natale stopped. Dead ahead, two men kneeled before the flame of Christ's candle.

212

Pietro spun about.

Giorgio did not move. "Go to him," he said. "Kiss his feet."

"Pa." He reached out for the old man's hand as he got up from the dirt. "You do not know me." He swallowed the sob in his throat. "Don't cry, Pa," he said in English, "I'm okay." He dropped his arms over the old man's shoulders and hid his face in the thick white hair.

He stepped back for his father to see him. "You look pretty good, Pa." He smiled. "A little older than before, that is all." He wiped his eyes on the sleeves of his white shirt. "Mario sends you his regards, Pa. Zia Emilia does not know I am here."

Giorgio slowly rose to his feet. "He is very happy to see you," he said quietly to Pietro, "with all the pain of this meeting."

Natale nodded his head, his face streaked with the tears of twenty years, and touched the tips of his fingers to Pietro's lips.

"Pa, what is it?"

And then the collector slammed his hands to his mouth to stifle the cry that broke from his throat like the lament of a stricken dog.

"Pa. What has been done to you?" Pietro screamed.

"He has given you his blessing," Giorgio said. "Go back now to the country of your birth."